Missing
Sammy

Missing Sammy

LINDA HUDSON HOAGLAND

Jan-Carol
Publishing, Inc

"every story needs a book"

MISSING SAMMY

LINDA HUDSON HOAGLAND

Published September 2015
Little Creek Books
Imprint of Jan-Carol Publishing, Inc
All rights reserved
Copyright © 2015 by Linda Hudson Hoagland

ISBN: 978-1-939289-74-2
Library of Congress Control Number: 2015953142

You may contact the publisher:
Jan-Carol Publishing, Inc
PO Box 701
Johnson City, TN 37605
publisher@jancarolpublishing.com
jancarolpublishing.com

To My Sons
Michael E. Hudson
Matthew A. Hudson

DEAR READER

This is a fact-based fiction journey through the life of Ella, a writer, a wife, a mother, an employee, a retiree; and finally, a happy woman. She found a light at the end of the tunnel, but it took surviving a long, hard fought battle to get there.

Eventually, everyone has to face the very same problems that Ella had to overcome. If nothing else, this books gives you hope.

Ella discovered that caring for her husband took all of her time outside of work and she did not allow friends to borrow, or use, any of her time. That was a mistake. When he passed on she had no close friends and she truly needed them. She had to build bridges to close the gaps of not being around those friends. Ella learned the hard way that women must make sure to keep those friendship ties.

Ella retired and loved it. It freed her up to do what she wanted to do.

Sincerely,
Linda Hoagland

INTRODUCTION

Ella is not the only widow in the world to have survived the death of a loved one. She knows that and she doesn't want people to consider her weak, so she fights for her self-control at all times around the public.

In the privacy of her home she battles through loneliness, depression, and the need to end it all. However, with the help of her friends Ella discovers she likes her life and finds a way to draw on the strength of the Appalachian roots she knew she could rely on, to bring her back to life.

CHAPTER 1
WHAT IF…

Ella was a writer. What she wrote was real life, much too real for the average, normal reader. At least, that's what she was told when her first book was released. So, she lightened up a bit and jumped headlong into mysteries. Strangely enough, mysteries and thrillers became her chosen genre.

"Okay, Maybelle, we're tackling a new story today. It's one that will cause the readers who get to actually absorb these pages to drop their jaws in open-mouthed amazement," she said to her computer. She caressed the keys, forming the words appearing on the screen.

Ella had learned many years earlier that the story she breathed life into with her words and her computer, which she affectionately called Maybelle, would eventually come true in way or another. That was her secret power, and she wielded it carefully so as not to do damage to someone who didn't deserve it.

Ella discovered this power with her second novel.

Her first novel was about events, most of which were true, that had already happened; not so with her second novel. Although her story was based on real people, the situations were different, and so were the names.

When she wrote in her second book that the Thompson home place would burn to the ground, it was only an idea in her brain.

When she discovered that the burning had occurred, she was shocked. Not to mention the fact that she was grateful the book hadn't been published before the burning.

She also mentioned the destruction of the vacant house on the hill, opposite the old school house. Those two structures also burned to the ground.

Had she caused that loss of those three Thompson landmarks? Was she responsible for the complete and total destruction of her family's structural ties to that piece of rocky, mountainous land?

Ella didn't think so, but what if...

"Who will we pick on today?" she asked her brightly-lit computer screen.

Of course, there was no response from the machine was spread out before her, thrusting its eye into the world of the Internet for everyone to see.

The software logo was gliding slowly across the screen, mesmerizing her. She sat staring at the screen. She didn't see it but her gaze was riveted to the steady movement, with her eyes being the only part of her body that moved perceptively.

Her mind was working, probing, and prodding at memories that could be molded and shaped into a new story to bring to life and possibly for publication, but that was her second thought.

"Maybelle, I think we're going to try to be nice today. I don't want to cause anybody any pain, not that I ever did. At least, I don't think I ever wanted to cause any trouble," she told her computer.

She found herself talking to her computer more and more often. It was safer that way. She was afraid that if she shared her innermost thoughts with the outside world, meaning not just with her computer, that someone might want to punish her for them after those very same thoughts became a reality.

Ella knew the whole entire world did not believe in her very special ability. As a matter of fact, she didn't either, not at the beginning.

Coincidence—that was what she wanted to call it. But after the coincidences continued to pile up, she knew better.

Was she foretelling the truth, or was she merely following the logical paths to the predictable outcomes? She hoped and prayed it was logic. That was the solution her mind could handle without fear, especially since her husband, Sammy, was no longer traveling with her.

Predicting or foretelling the future could lead her down dangerous roads, perhaps thrusting life-threatening curves and side routes in front of her before she could actually reach the end. She knew that for a fact. It had happened to her many times.

Ella had heard the following statement many times from people who were reading a book or watching a movie: "I hate it when someone gives away the ending." That was the same way she felt when she knew the outcome before she actually got to sink her teeth into the story.

Did Ella make these events happen? Were they real, or just part of her overactive imagination?

The truth of the matter was that she was confusing fact and fiction, she thought.

CHAPTER 2
FOR THE LOVE OF SNAKES

Ella watched him; he was sitting on one of those extremely uncomfortable blue chairs in the waiting room. There was something about him, something she just couldn't put her finger on, that made her sneak a peek at him every time she raised her head from staring at her typewriter.

He had a pleasant face, a medium build, and medium blonde hair, a lock or two of which kept falling forward, forcing him to brush it back.

He had asked to see Mr. Burton, her boss, the best attorney in town, about filing for a divorce. As sad as the idea of divorce should seem to anyone, inwardly Ella was happy about the thought that he would be available.

He was talking to another man who had come into the lobby with him. The other man, who turned out to be Sammy's brother, Dave, was unhappy about not being able to drink his can of beer. It was sitting in the car getting warm. Dave fidgeted and squirmed in his chair much like an impatient child.

Ella didn't think either one of them saw her sneaking peeks; at least, she hoped they didn't.

Dave stood up and angrily told Sammy, by whom she was mesmerized, that he would be waiting in the car.

"Good riddance, you're drunk," she heard Sammy whisper as Dave walked out of the room.

"Do you know how much longer it will be before I can talk to Mr. Burton?" he asked, standing in front of Ella's desk.

"I'm sorry, sir, but Mr. Burton is with another client. It shouldn't be much longer," Ella said as kindly as she could. She knew people hated to wait.

"My name is Sammy," he said with a smile.

"My name is Ella. Would you like to look at a magazine?" she asked, trying to get him to talk to her. "I'll get one for you, if you like."

A few moments later, she heard Mr. Burton come to the doorway, to walk the client with whom he had been speaking through the lobby. He held the door for him as the client exited the room. He gently closed the door and looked at Sammy.

"Are you here to see me?" he asked Sammy.

"If you're Mr. Burton. Yes sir, I'm here to see you," said Sammy.

"Come on into my office. We'll get you started," said Mr. Burton.

Ella watched Sammy and Mr. Burton leave the reception area. Her mind was running in overdrive. How was she going to get to know Sammy? There was just something about him.

Several days passed before she saw Sammy again. She had to call him to schedule an appointment for him to sign the divorce papers before they were filed in court. At the very least, she had his telephone number, even if she was too old-fashioned to use it for her own purposes. To her way of thinking, the man should make the first move.

When he entered the lobby for his newly scheduled appointment, his face lit up with sunshine when he said hello to Ella. His bright blue eyes sparkled with merriment, accented by fine lines of age that formed a starburst of happiness. His smile matched his eyes.

Ella knew she turned every shade of red as she wondered how hard she had been concentrating on getting him to ask her out for a date.

She knew he had four children, ranging in ages from elementary school to high school. Ella also had two boys in middle school.

Mr. Burton took Sammy into his office right away, so she didn't get a chance to talk with him. On his way past her desk and out the door, Sammy whispered for her to call him. Ella nodded in acknowledgment of his request.

"I can't call Sammy," she told herself, as she thought about his request.

***

Ella was daydreaming about what to do next when the telephone rang. Her eldest son was on the line.

"Mom, we have snakes under the house!" he said excitedly.

"What?" Ella asked.

"Mrs. Johnson said she saw a great, big, old copperhead crawl under our house," he explained.

"You and Aaron stay in the house, Eddy, and don't go to the back yard. I'll see if anyone knows how to get rid of snakes. Okay?" Ella said apprehensively.

"All right, but do something, will you?" he pleaded.

No one was in the office for Ella to ask for snake ridding instructions so she called Sammy. She had read the notes in Sammy's file and discovered that Sammy's wife had been stepping out on him, looking for a bigger and better provider. He actually caught her in his bed with another man.

Ella knew that after the second appointment with Mr. Burton, she would never see him or talk to him again. She had to come up with a problem he could help her solve. A telephone call from her son provided the problem and a call from Ella to Sammy would provide the solution, she hoped.

"Sammy Holcombe, please," she said into the telephone.

"I'm Sammy."

"Hi, I'm Ella Hutchins. You probably don't remember me, but..."

"Sure, you're Mr. Burton's secretary. How are you?" he asked in a not-too-confident tone. "Is there a problem with the divorce?"

"No, no, no divorce problem. Do you know how to get rid of snakes?" Ella sputtered into the telephone.

"What? Snakes? Who is this again?" he shouted back at her.

"Never mind," she said quietly. "I'll find out from someone else. I'll just say goodbye and we can forget this conversation ever happened," she said as she tried to end the phone call without embarrassing herself any further.

"No! No, please don't hang up. I'm glad you called. Where are the snakes?" asked Sammy.

"Under my house, and I just wanted to see if you know how to get a snake from under a house," she answered in explanation.

"What kind of snake?" he asked with a smile in his tone.

"My son told me it was a copperhead," Ella said

"I really don't know what to tell you, without looking around the place. Is it your house?" he asked.

"Yes," she answered.

"How old are your kids?" Sammy asked.

"Eddy is twelve, and Aaron is ten," Ella answered.

"Tell them to stay away from the snake. The bite of a copperhead might not kill you, but it will make you pretty sick. Do you want me to come to your house and check it out? I don't know if I can do anything, but I will give it a try," Sammy said.

"That would be great, Sammy. The boys would feel better if they had someone other than me telling them not to worry about the snake. I should get off work in about an hour. I'll meet you there," Ella said with excitement.

She gave him her address, and he found her house without a problem. Of course, there was nothing he could do about the snake except tell the boys to keep a watchful eye out for the creepy-crawly.

***

"Ella, I made the last payment on our rings today. See, here's the receipt," said Sammy as he proudly displayed the small, yellow receipt with PAID IN FULL written in bold letters across it.

"Where are they?" Ella asked.

"Right here," he said as he plunged his hand into his jacket extracting the blue, velvet-lined box. "When can we get married?"

"Soon, real soon," said Ella as she opened the box to look at the shiny, golden rings.

"What about next week?" asked Sammy.

"Okay, but we've got to buy our license and then we have to wait three days," explained Ella.

"It won't be anything fancy. Nothing like what you're entitled to," Sammy whispered apologetically.

"It doesn't have to be fancy, Honey. We love each other, and that's all we need," said Ella softly.

"Are you going to take any time off work?" asked Sammy.

"I can't. Mr. Burton is going to be out of town for about a month, and I have to help him tie up loose ends before he leaves. You know what a busy lawyer he is," Ella answered sadly.

"What are we going to do?" Sammy asked, guessing that the wedding was going to be delayed again.

"We'll get our marriage license Monday, during the lunch hour. Then we'll drive five miles to New Boston, to be married by the mayor, on Friday during lunch. I've already checked with the mayor's office," said Ella.

They had been planning to get married for three months. In August they had put a small down payment on their rings, having decided to be married on September 16th, which was the 39th wedding anniversary of her parents.

A couple of days after the down payment was made, Ella was told that her father had cancer and would only have a few months to live.

Their marriage plans were completely halted when her father's health moved quickly from bad to worse. The money that was intended to pay for the rings was used for other expenses, and the bedside vigil took precedence over the frivolity of wedding preparations.

On September 16th, the day Sammy and Ella had planned to be married, her father succumbed to cancer.

Almost a month later, they were excited again about being able to get married. They had decided to tell no one, just in case something else happened to force them to change their plans again.

"Ella?" said Sammy.

"Sammy, what's the matter? Why aren't you on your way here to pick me up?" asked a concerned Ella.

"The car won't start," Sammy said sullenly.

"Oh," said Ella.

"What do you want me to do now?" Sammy asked.

"Just get it fixed. We'll go tomorrow. There will still be enough time. Don't worry, okay? Just get the car fixed," Ella said, as she tried to be cheerful.

Ella went through the remainder of Monday at work like a lost soul. Even though she had encouraged Sammy with cheerful words, she was so afraid something else would go wrong.

Tuesday was the day to get the license.

Sammy picked Ella up and they drove the five miles to New Boston, completed the necessary paperwork, and grabbed a quick sandwich before Ella returned to work.

"Where'd you go for lunch?" asked Thelma.

"We grabbed a hamburger and drove around for a while," said Ella, nonchalantly.

"Oh, I thought you might have done something different," added Thelma as she was leaving the room.

Ella smiled and went about her work. She was so happy about getting married, finally, that she wanted to share the feeling with the world.

Her happy feeling was replaced with nervous anticipation that caused her mind to jump around. Concentrating on work became a difficult task. Sleeping that night was even harder to do. Her mind had covered every possible mishap, from the car not starting again to her having a heart attack.

When the alarm rang Friday morning, she jumped out of bed, checking to see that she was not having chest pains.

Ella picked out one of her nicer outfits to wear, keeping in mind that she still had to go to work. She called Sammy so she could hear his voice, and make sure everything was going smoothly so far.

"Hi, Honey," Ella said into the receiver after she heard his sleepy hello.

"Is there anything wrong, Ella?" he asked worriedly.

"No, everything is fine. Everything is perfect. I just wanted to hear your voice, and tell you that I love you," cooed Ella.

"I love you, too," replied Sammy.

"I'll see you at noon. I love you, Sammy," she whispered.

"Love you, too," he said.

Ella replaced the telephone receiver and went to her car.

"Nellie, don't fail me now," she prayed as she turned the ignition key to start her car. When the engine roared to life she was relieved. Now her only worry was that Sammy's car wouldn't start.

"Ella, you want to go to lunch with Amy and me?" asked Thelma.

"No, I can't. Sammy is picking me up," Ella answered cheerfully.

"Again? Where are you going this time?" asked Thelma.

"New Boston," answered Ella.

"You going to the steak house?" probed Thelma.

"Yes, I may be a little late. Will you cover for me?" Ella answered, hoping Thelma would end the inquisition.

"Sure, no problem. Have a good lunch," Thelma said as she walked out the door.

When Sammy pulled up to the curb in front of the building, Ella jumped into the car and kissed him before he had a chance to say hello.

They were on their way.

At the mayor's office, they waited a few minutes while the mayor, who was also a minister, readied himself for the short service.

The actual marriage ceremony took only five minutes, and the pep talk issued by the mayor was short and sweet.

When Sammy and Ella left the mayor's office, they were husband and wife. They were each wearing a beautiful, golden wedding band that bound them together forever.

"Sammy, we've got to stop at the steak house," Ella giggled.

"Why? We don't have time to eat. You have to get back to work," said Sammy.

"I know, but I told Thelma that was where I was going, and I want to make sure it wasn't a lie. All I want to do is walk through the front door then turn around and leave," Ella explained.

"You're crazy, Ella," said Sammy as he smiled at his new wife.

"No, Honey, just honest," Ella responded.

When Ella arrived at work, she was about fifteen minutes late.

"Did you have a good lunch?" questioned Thelma.

"Sure did," Ella replied as she flagrantly waved her left hand in front of Thelma.

"What's that?" asked Thelma as she pointed at Ella's left hand.

"What?" asked Ella, faking surprise.

"On your left hand!" asked Thelma.

"That's my wedding band. I just got married," said Ella, trying to hold back her excitement.

"You're kidding," said Thelma.

"No, I'm now Mrs. Sammy Holcombe, and the happiest woman alive."

The lunch hour wedding occurred in 1983. It was her third marriage, and his second. Sammy and Ella remained together for twenty-five years, but not for the love of snakes.

CHAPTER 3
A HOUSE FOR CHRISTMAS

Ella's anniversary (eighteenth to be exact) came and went in October. No celebration was had, no gifts received, no notice was taken, no tears of happiness for an unexpected surprise were shed. She gritted her teeth, said a little prayer, and proceeded to get through the day.

Ella's fifty-third birthday passed in early November without any fanfare and, again, no material recognition. She received no card, no telephone call, nothing, from her sons or husband. She was disappointed but finally, after all of the years of nothing, she'd learned to shrug it off and lived through another normal day.

It was routine for her family not to remember her on her special days. It had become her job over the years, reminding everyone of upcoming birthdays and reasons for celebration with regard to everyone except Ella. When she chose not to remind anyone of her birthday or Mother's Day or their anniversary, Ella gave up her rights to remembrance. She didn't like it, but it was not an unusual occurrence for her to be passed by and forgotten. She knew it wasn't intentional, and she guessed it was partly her fault, because she always reminded others so they wouldn't have to think about it of their own accord. Ella wanted to avoid the pain of being forgotten by the person whose special event was being celebrated. She only wanted to help, not hinder. She shrugged, said a little prayer, and smiled as each one of her special events passed her by without any kind of fanfare.

Ella was usually not on the receiving end of any type of remembrance, but heaven forbid she should pass up any type of special day for her two grown sons or her overgrown child of a husband. They each and every one would stand in front of her with outstretched hands when their special days arrived. They expected the recognition and celebration, especially for their birthdays, that she had lavished on each of them for years. If she couldn't give the special guy a material extravagance, she gave him everything she could scrape up and throw together, from a card, to a cake, to a party, to a special gift. Ella did everything she could to make that person feel special on his own special day. They did feel special and loved, which was her special plan.

Ella was sure it was in the genes. She didn't program them to remember anniversaries, birthdays, and so on. They were programmed to take action only when reminded to do so, by her. She didn't remind them anymore of her days, or her need to be recognized and loved, so it was her fault. She had to grit her teeth, say a little prayer, shrug her shoulders, and smile so she could get on with her day.

Sammy and Ella had watched their children reach adulthood and evolve into good people with lives of their own. They were left with each other, and wanted a better life for the two of them because they felt they'd earned it.

This year Ella was not going to let the thoughtless neglect by her loved ones bother her, because Christmas was coming. It was going to be a better Christmas than any they'd ever known or ever expected to have. She knew she wouldn't have to grit her teeth, say a little prayer, shrug, smile, and try to forget.

They were getting a house for Christmas.

It started with the urging of her friend, Pat, for Ella to submit an application to the Stillwell County Habitat for Humanity, over a year earlier.

The process for approval was time-consuming for the Habitat's volunteers, and the wait for a house could take years. Funds must be garnered, volunteers wrangled, and the weather had to cooperate before the first nail could driven.

During the period of waiting, Ella and Sammy moved out of their dilapidated mobile home, where rain was leaking in onto the wiring that hooked into the breaker box. They were afraid they would be burned up or burned out of their home, with nothing to show for their years of toil. They moved into a rental home, located twenty miles closer to her place of employment. Distance from work was no problem for Sammy, because he was disabled. They continued to wait, with only a glimmer of distant hope to hang on to for support.

The Habitat for Humanity home that had been built in Stillwell three years earlier was occupied by a young mother, who later married and wanted to start her new life with her new husband in a new and different home. She left the Habitat home to be recycled, resold to waiting applicants.

Ella wanted to thank all of those who allowed their names and number to pop up, which gave them an opportunity to thrust their roots into the ground. They no longer were members of the transient society in Stillwell County, who lived in mobile homes and rental dwellings.

They gladly started the process of fixing up, painting, and getting ready to move into their Christmas present, which would be like no other they'd ever receive in their lifetimes.

They were in their home by Christmas and no other thoughts, wishes, or presents were necessary.

They had to wait four long months, during which time they paid rent to Stillwell County Habitat for Humanity, before they closed on the house and actually got a piece of paper telling them they were actual homeowners.

Ella didn't think the dream of owning a house would ever come true because their ages were rapidly adding up. Their income was becoming stationary but their expenses, especially medical, were multiplying. Besides, the price of real estate was rising much, much faster than their income.

Until she got that piece of paper that told her, Sammy, and the world that they were homeowners, she didn't feel comfortable. She was afraid it was a dream, and that she would wake up and it would be gone.

She finally received that piece of paper.

Ella thanked Stillwell County Habitat for Humanity and God for allowing them to fulfill a dream, because when she woke up, that piece of paper was still there.

Come one, come all, to the first Habitat home in Stillwell County, Virginia. They don't have much, but what they do have, they will share.

CHAPTER 4
THOSE HABITAT PEOPLE

Dust was everywhere, but it wasn't only dust that marred the image before Ella. The dirt, grime, and filth that had been allowed to accumulate in a short period of time, less than a year, was unbelievable.

"Ella, we would like for you and Sammy to do most of the cleaning of the house in Duran. It was built last year, and the people who were buying the house were made to move out and relinquish the title for nonpayment," said Jane. She was in charge of keeping track of the equity hours for the Habitat's recipients.

"Sure, we would be happy to help," Ella said.

"You'll be doing most of the cleanup work alone, because no one else is available. Is that a problem?" asked Jane.

"No, should it be?" asked Ella.

"You can answer that when you see the place, Ella. You need to wear old clothes, the kind you can throw out after wearing them one more time," warned Jane.

"How old is this house?" asked Ella.

"Less than a year. I'll have someone meet you there with a key on Saturday. What time do you think you'll get there?" said Jane, changing the subject quickly.

"About eight in the morning. I like to get an early start," Ella said, apprehensively.

When Ella's mind went back to that conversation, she realized that Jane had been trying to warn her about what she was getting into. Even if she had understood the warning, she wouldn't have believed a mother with two young children and their disabled, wheelchair-bound grandfather could have caused the amount of havoc and destruction they'd accomplished while living in a brand new house.

As Ella's eyes took in all the sights to be seen, she realized why no one else was available to help clean the house. Sammy and Ella were the newest kids on the block, in this county. In order to gain possession of their house, they had to clean, paint, and repair the structure after the previous owners had returned the ownership of the house to the builders, Stillwell County Habitat for Humanity.

The task Sammy and Ella took on in order to earn their house was minimal in comparison with what they were facing with their new assignment. In order to get their house; they had to clean baseboards, walls, shelves, and anything else that could be improved with soap and water. Then they were given gallons of paint, rollers, and brushes, and were told to make the house the way they'd want it to be to live in it.

Their own house simply required the removal of signs of the previous family, which consisted of the single mother with two little girls. There was no major destruction, only the wear and tear that the family living in a home caused. Their biggest worry was trying to get the color scheme in each of the rooms to fade away and die. Yellow seemed to be a favorite in every room, with the exception of one wall in each room that was painted an unusually dark color ,such as navy blue. But they did it; it turned out beautifully, with a lot of effort on their part. Joy and happiness exuded from their pores, because they were actually getting a house of their very own.

"Sammy, how could they do this? How could they treat such a wonderful opportunity as if it were an insult and punishment?" Ella asked, tears streaming from her eyes.

Sammy shrugged as he looked around. He didn't have an answer for the abuse of a good thing.

A car pulled up onto the gravel driveway, disgorging a couple of people who walked through the front door looking angry and upset.

"I'm Ella and this is my husband, Sammy. Are you here to help?" asked Ella.

"This is supposed to be our house. Why are you here?" demanded a young woman who was probably in her early twenties.

"We came to clean. Don't you want us to help?" asked Sammy.

He received no answer, other than a glaring stare from across the room.

"Sammy, let's get started," Ella whispered so that only he could hear. "We need to get out of here as soon as we can."

Now, keep in mind that this house was less than a year old when reading what they had to do to clean it up.

"Sammy, we're going to need a shovel to find the carpet in the living room," said Ella.

"The Habitat repair trailer is out back. Maybe there's one in there," said Sammy.

While he was outside trying to break into the trailer because he couldn't find the key, Ella tried to jump-start a conversation with the sad, new, future owners of the mess they were trying to clean up.

"What's your name?" Ella asked, hoping she would receive something other than a glaring stare in response.

"I'm Sandy and that's my husband, Dave. It's my mom and dad who are getting this house. It's a mess. I don't know how those Habitat people they think we can live in a mess like this," she said sullenly.

There was no doubt that she and her husband were not happy. They weren't too anxious about attacking the mess that was strewn all through the house.

"I thought you said your mom and dad were going to live here. That doesn't matter because it will look just like new when we get finished. Don't worry about how it looks now," Ella explained.

"How can you make this mess disappear? How can anyone want to live here?" asked Sandy.

"Why don't you guys start in the back bedroom? Sammy and I will do the kitchen and the living room. All we are required to do is clean up and splash on a few gallons of this cover-up paint. Habitat will make sure all major repair jobs are completed to your satisfaction, or that of your mother and father. I'm sure by the time this place is finished, it will look like new," Ella said through clenched teeth.

"It can't possibly look new ever again," Sandy said. She stomped out of the room and out the front door.

Sammy and Ella worked hard for long hours as they shoveled, swept, and then vacuumed the floors. Ella tackled the kitchen appliances, which were caked with burnt-on food and grime. The refrigerator was a disaster for the nose. Food had been allowed to remain inside when there was no electricity, so all kinds of molds and fungi were spreading happily to cover every surface.

Ella crawled inside cabinets, wiping them clean, while Sammy tackled closets and once again, started loading up garbage bags.

The previous owners, it was rumored, had been involved with drugs. Part of the ceiling in one of the bedrooms was caving in where a person had climbed into the area to either hide himself or heavy containers of whatever your imagination allowed you to see. Ella was inclined to believe it was a human being hidden from the legal authorities.

The walls, all of them, were covered with crayon, permanent marker, and nail polish child high. No amount of scrubbing and elbow grease would remove the destruction that was allowed to roam through the house in the form of neglected children. It would take more than one coat of cover-up paint, several coats was Ella's guess.

It wasn't their house. They had their house. They were treating this house as if it were going to come into their hands, so they worked very hard to make it presentable to the new owners.

This work was all volunteer; well, not exactly all. They felt obligated to accomplish their goal, but if they had been physically unable to do the job, they would not have been chastised in any way. They felt they needed to do this to thank the Stillwell County Habitat for Humanity for giving them a chance.

It took them a couple of weekends but when they were finished; all the new owners had to do was paint the walls the colors they preferred. Habitat had furnished new carpet and all of the repair work necessary to make the house like the new home that it was.

In her heart, Ella still found it difficult to understand why anyone would allow a brand new house to be destroyed like the previous owners had. Also, she found it hard to understand how the family members of the new owners could be so critical and resentful of the golden opportunity to improve the family's living conditions when some hard work might be involved. You had to earn the right to own a Habitat home.

Sammy and Ella earned their right to own their house without resentment. They hoped that others would feel as they did, continue to work to earn their own houses, and be grateful for the opportunity that had been given to them.

CHAPTER 5
GREEN

Ella wasn't especially prone to nightmares, so she was really surprised when she started having them. She didn't have a reappearance of terror every night, but the one she remembered most occurred in basically the same form, quite often. It seemed to be like reruns on television. The same nightmare played itself out the exact same way, every time the film started in her head.

Ella should have taken it for the warning it was.

***

"Pull over to the side of the road, Sammy, I want to get a piece of the plant growing there," Ella said, urging him to do exactly what he didn't want to do.

"Ella, you don't need that. You've got plenty of plants growing all over the house," he said, in a disgusted tone of voice.

"Pull over, Sammy. I really do want a piece of that plant. It's so pretty and green, with strong, healthy-looking vines. It would really look great growing up the side of our little house. It might hide some of the flaws left by neglect, if you know what I mean," Ella said a little more harshly than she should have.

"All right, all right, but you still don't need it," he growled with a smile.

Ella climbed out of the car and broke off a couple of snippets at the leaf joint. The lush green plant was growing over the naked, cut stone on the side of the road. Greenery was **plan**ted in certain areas to facilitate the holding back of the rubble so it wouldn't fall onto passing cars, she was told.

As soon as she reached the confines of her small kitchen, Ella filled a pint-sized Mason jar with water and lovingly placed the twigs of green into the sparkling cold liquid. When the water was introduced, the leaves proceeded to take in the water like humans would take in a big gulp of air. The leaves seemed to stand straighter and spread themselves further into the world, because they were being given a second chance at life. Ella placed the jar on the window-sill in the sunlight over the kitchen sink, so she could check the progress of growth. She wanted to be sure it was forming the necessary roots before planting the new greenery at the side of the house, where the brown earth was determined to show itself.

Ella never thought about the new plant life on her window-sill for a couple of days. She was near the kitchen sink several times, but she knew, under normal circumstances, she would not see roots peeking out of the green stems for at least a week, if not longer. Not so for the new green addition. Long, white tendrils were dangling from each stem, indicating that it was time to remove them from the life sustaining water and gingerly place them into the brown earth, allowing the green snippets to grow into lush, green visions of beauty for all passersby to behold.

"Hey, Sammy, look at my plant cuttings. They are ready to plant into the ground," Ella shouted excitedly.

Of course, laid-back Sammy had no idea why she was so excited.

"What is it you want me to see?" he asked.

She held the Mason jar up to the bright sunlight of the window and pointed at the white, silky roots.

"So-o-o-o-," he said, not having any idea that he was witnessing something unusual.

"They grew so fast. Plants don't usually take root that quickly," Ella said as she placed the jar back onto the windowsill. "I'll try to get them into the dirt at the side of the house as soon as I get home from work tomorrow. Then we'll see how quickly they'll grow in the fresh, clean soil that will be surrounding their silky roots."

When Ella arrived home from work the next day she grabbed the Mason jar, along with her garden spade, and made her way to the green plant's new home. The ground was hard from the lack of water. Rain had been scarce for the last few days, but she kept digging at it, breaking it up. Eventually she got the holes deep enough to set the plants far enough down into the loosely packed earth to cover all the white tendrils, leaving only the upper portion of the stem and leaves exposed to the bright sunlight.

After carefully patting down the loose soil, she fetched her watering can. Ella had already mixed in the liquid fertilizer she was going to use to add a little boost to the nutrients the plants would get from the soil. She poured the water only on the dirt, because she was afraid the chemicals of the fertilizer might damage the beautiful, green leaves.

The plants were right outside her bedroom window, but because they were so tiny at this point, Ella would have to go outside and walk around to the side of the house to check on the growth progress.

She got busy and forgot to check for two days. She ran to the bedroom window, opened the mini blinds, and jerked up the window. She was in the process of changing from her work clothes into something casual, so she could pull some weeds from her flower bed.

"Oh, my God," Ella whispered.

The tiny little green snippets had branched out into several long, lanky, rope-like tentacles, grasping at any crack or crevice the tentacles could reach. As Ella stood watching, she thought she could actually see the vine growing, getting longer and reaching for new heights to climb. It was almost like watching time-lapse photography that had been speeded up to show the growth cycle of a plant in a manner of seconds.

Before Ella exited her bedroom, she closed the mini blinds but left the window open a bit to let in some much-needed fresh air.

"Hey, Sammy. Let's go outside and check out the new plants," Ella shouted. She wrestled her feet into her tennis shoes, which she had carried into the living room.

They walked hand in hand to the side of the house, where he said, "Look at that, Ella. Are those the plants you put there a couple of days ago?"

Ella shook her head and laughed at the surprise that was registering on his face.

"What do you think?" Ella asked.

"I've never seen anything like that, Ella. What did you put on those things?" asked Sammy.

"Liquid fertilizer and water. That's all," answered Ella.

"Well, you'll have what you wanted in a couple of days, not a couple of months as you thought would happen," commented Sammy.

"Yes, I guess so. I wanted the flaws of neglect hidden, but I didn't want them completely overtaken," said Ella.

Sammy went back inside. Ella remained outside, so she could pull the renegade weeds from the flower beds in front of the house.

Bedtime rolled around, and Ella was ready. She had worked herself up to the point of being beyond tired. Much to her surprise, she couldn't sleep. She tossed and turned. She finally reached the point of giving up with the bed, and moved into the living room to stretch out on the sofa in front of the television, so it would lull her to sleep.

That didn't work, either. Something was nagging at her brain, teasing it, like it was dangling just out of reach. She couldn't grab hold of the thought.

She knew Sammy was okay. He was snoring when she left the bedroom. He almost always slept soundly, due to all of the drugs he had to take for his failing heart.

Ella dozed off and all she could see was green. Why green?

She heard no sounds other than the soft drone of the television. Why couldn't she sleep? If she fell into slumber, why couldn't she continue? Ella would wake up with a jerk, and listen. What was she listening for? A crawling sound, maybe?

Ella finally gave up at six o'clock. She made a mad dash for the bathroom, passing her bedroom with its door wide open on the way. She hadn't turned on any lights, and was using only the nightlights for illumination. Something didn't look right, but Mother Nature was pressuring her to walk on by, permitting her only a glance.

When Ella completed her bathroom task, she returned to the hallway, flicked on the overhead light, and screamed.

Green was slithering across her carpet in the hallway, like hundreds of writhing snakes. When she looked directly at the green, there was no movement. When she averted her head, allowing only her peripheral vision to encompass the green, she could see movement ever so slightly.

The mass of green was coming from her bedroom, where Sammy was sleeping.

Why didn't he wake me up?

"Sammy!" screamed Ella.

No answer. Just the slight whispery sound of something crawling across the carpet.

"Sammy, wake up!" Ella screamed again.

She reached into the laundry basket of folded clothes from the night before, yanking out some underclothes along with her jeans and a tee-shirt. She ran down the hallway to the kitchen and reached for the telephone.

Ella didn't know dialing 9-1-1 was so difficult. She had to make herself stop and re-enter the numbers twice before she could get it right.

"My husband, there is something wrong with my husband," Ella shouted into the telephone.

"What's the problem, Ma'am?" asked the 9-1-1 operator.

"He isn't answering me," shouted Ella.

"Is he breathing?" asked the 9-1-1 operator.

"I don't know. I'm afraid to go into the bedroom," said Ella, a little less loudly.

"Why?" asked the 9-1-1 operator.

"The plant is coming after me. I'm afraid it's already killed my husband," Ella said, in almost a whisper.

Ella knew she sounded crazy. She wasn't going to worry about that. Maybe that would make them move a little faster.

"You might want to send the police chief and the ambulance," Ella said as she hung up the telephone.

The green had interrupted its path towards the living room, and rerouted itself towards the kitchen. Was it looking for heat? The warmth of her body? Was it looking for blood? Was it following the sound of her voice?

"I don't know what it wants, but I'm getting out of here," Ella mumbled.

She ran to the front door, wrestled with the door lock, and ran outside, screaming her head off. She wanted the whole world to know there was a monster inside her house.

When the ambulance arrived, the paramedics would not enter the house until the police arrived.

They waited.

The green found its way to the front door and started making its way outside. It seemed to be trying to enshroud Ella's little house beneath its deadly vines and leaves.

"Look! Look at that!" Ella said as she pointed at the slithering growth. "It's coming after me."

The stunned paramedics backed up with Ella, trying to get away from the green.

The police chief pulled up with sirens screaming and lights flashing.

"What's going on here?" he shouted.

"Look over there. That plant is coming after us," shouted the paramedics as they scrambled to get to their ambulance and move it further down the street.

"Who lives here?" shouted the police chief.

"I do. We do. My husband and I," Ella answered loudly. She stood on the street, staring back at the green monster.

"Where is your husband?" he asked calmly.

"Inside. I think he might be dead," Ella said, as she tried to hold back the tears.

The police chief started shouting orders over the radio. Soon there were a couple more police cars with lights flashing, parked on the street blocking traffic.

The officers exited the vehicles with large, heavy scythes.

"Where does this growth start?" he asked harshly.

"At the side of the house. I just planted it there less than a week ago. It grew from two tiny clippings. What kind of plant is it?" Ella answered.

"We received a bulletin about it this morning. It's a mutated species of kudzu. It is designed for rapid growth and ground cover," explained the police chief.

"What feeds it?" Ella asked incredulously.

"Anything in its path."

The scythes cut away the roots and then the police officers started pulling the detached vines out of the house. Had they killed the roots completely?

They uncovered Sammy's body, and it was generally believed that he died peacefully in his sleep due to a heart attack.

That wasn't what Ella believed.

***

Ella woke up covered with sweat, and reached out for the feel of Sammy's warm body, lying on the bed sleeping peacefully. The rhythm of his breathing calmed her, and lulled her back to a dreamless sleep.

Death could happen at any time, for any reason. Ella knew that, and she hoped her dream wasn't telling her that her Sammy would die when she was least expecting it.

CHAPTER 6
IN SAMMY'S WORDS

My name is Sammy Holcombe. Please understand that I am not a good speller and that means I often spell towns, cities, and people's names incorrectly. Ella corrected everything she could, but since she didn't live my life, she didn't know what was wrong.

Also, in some places I changed the names of some people because I didn't want any hard feelings. So forgive me if you received this book and you thought the story included you as a participant, where I labeled you with a different name. Ella didn't know who all of you were.

I changed the names to protect me, you, and Ella because I loved you all.

People who have written a book said there's a book in everyone, at least, that was what my wife, Ella, kept telling me. She heard that from somewhere, but I don't know where.

She said you first have to sit down and write one. Well, that was harder than I thought, but I knew I had a good one in me.

My book started even before I was born. My father's father, mother, four brothers, and two sisters grew up in the Dayton and

Fairborn area, around the Wright Patterson Air Force Base in Ohio.

My grandfather's name was Wayne Samuel Holston, and my grandma's name was Gertrude Eileen. Grandpa worked at Wright Patterson Air Force Base. My dad's name was Vern, and his brothers' names were Lester, Robert, Lonnie, and Ralph. Their sisters were Eileen and Dorothy.

Along the way, they moved into a home on Rheam Road, where grandpa became an indentured slave for some mysterious reason.

That was when all of the kids were separated; some went to the Children's Home. Vern was one of those who went to the Children's Home.

***

This was a story about my life, growing up with my family across from the Ohio River.

There were good times and bad times living there.

My name is Sammy Holcombe and I was born in Columbus, Ohio, at White Cross Hospital and it no longer exists.

My mother's name was Teresa M. Holcombe, with her maiden name being Key. My mother was raised in a Children's Home in Hillsboro, Ohio. My father was raised in the same Children's Home. In those days, things were very bad for many people.

My Uncles Lester and Robert lived with their Uncles, Lonnie and Ralph. The two boys helped with their uncles' farm. Some of the boys joined the service during World War II.

Grandpa Holston remained an indentured slave until Uncle Lester and Aunt Sandy went and rescued him. Lester worked at the Dayton Power and Light Company. Lester and Sandy had eight children.

When mom was old enough to run away from the home, she did so. I guess my dad did the same thing. Teresa, mom, got a job, then met and married a man named Glen Ernest. They had four kids, named John, Allison, Dave, and Betsy Ernest. Glen and Teresa were married for about six years. Glen was a drunk and didn't work. Teresa was finally fed up with him, and filed for a divorce. Teresa had to go to work, so she told Allison to stay home and watch Betsy while she was working. Allison would go out and run around with her friends instead. Allison was fourteen at the time. John and Dave would also be out running around. No one was caring for Betsy.

In 1942 Teresa, my mother, met my father, Vern Holcombe.

Dad was in the Armed Forces when they met. While dad was in the Army, he was a military police officer.

Vern and Teresa got married in 1944.

My parents moved to the southern part of Ohio, to a town called Manchester. They lived just outside of Manchester, about three miles. That was when I came along. I was born in 1947.

I had two half-brothers and two half-sisters, because we had different fathers.

When I had reached the age of five, Betsy and I would go outside to play in the front yard. Betsy and I would scare our mother to death all the time, because we had an Uncle Pete who would come drive to our house, pick us up, and take us to town to buy us some candy. Boy, did my mother get mad at my Uncle Pete.

In 1953, mom gave birth to my little brother, Rosco. He was the brother I never got to know.

One evening my Aunt Karen, Uncle Buck, and another man came to see mom and dad. I was almost six years old at the time, and I didn't know I had a little brother.

When my aunt, uncle, and the other man were in the next room and the door was closed, I was with all of my sisters and brothers in the dining room. I heard my mother crying really loud, and I thought something was wrong with her. When I heard mom crying, I started crying so loud that my brother got mad. He came over to me and slapped me hard across the face. I ran into the front room and crawled onto the sofa, where I fell asleep.

When I woke up the next morning, everything was quiet and everyone went about their business. It wasn't until I was eleven years old that I found out what really happened in that room, behind the closed door. The reason I found out was because I overheard my mom and my aunt talking about it. That's when I asked mom what happened.

She said I had a little brother who died in the room behind the closed door. My little brother was three months old when he died.

I didn't know John or Allison very well, because they were already out on their own. Dave and Betsy were still at home. Most of the time Dave was in the woods, walking around or hunting.

Some of our family came to our house to stay, because they had no other place to live. Their names were Harry and Evelyn Denson. They had three kids; Sarah, Raymond, and Ben.

Sometimes dad's brother and family would come to visit us. Their names were Lester and Lena Holcombe. We would have a picnic on Route 52, where Uncle Lonnie had some land. It was a good place to play, and we would eat there. The men would swing on the large grape vines, and the kids would swing on the smaller grapevines. Sometimes the men would try to put three men on the same vine at the same time. The vine would break and the men would fall to ground and hurt their butts. The women would be laughing themselves to death. By that time, we would all be hungry, so the women would have lunch ready to eat. After lunch we would sit around, then go down over the hill to the Ohio River to go swimming

My brother, John, almost drowned in the Ohio River at that time. John didn't know how to swim, and my Aunt Eileen saved him. Mom told me one time that my father swam from the Ohio side of the river to the Kentucky side, and back again. The Ohio River was about a mile across. She said no one else had ever done that.

One day while Raymond, Ben, and I were playing outside, Raymond decided to throw some sand in my eyes. I started to cry really loudly, because I couldn't see. Mom and Dad came over to where I was and wanted to know what was wrong. I told them what Raymond had done, and his father gave him the whipping of his life.

Our house was surrounded by woods. My mom would plant a garden every summer, but the Ohio River would flood and wash it away. Mom would work the garden by herself, because John and Allison were already gone. Dave was always in the woods hunting. Betsy and I were too young to help, and dad was at work most of the time.

CHAPTER 7
IN SAMMY'S WORDS—SNOWBALL

When my sister and I were little kids, we had a German shepherd dog, Snowball, which was of course white in color. Our German shepherd would do anything to protect us, from anyone and anything.

We lived on the outskirts of Manchester, Ohio, on Route 52 West, in a little white house across from the Ohio River. Our little white house was completely surrounded by woods.

When my sister and I would get into trouble, our mother would attempt to spank us but our German shepherd would get in between us, start to growl, and would not let our mother touch us. She would get mad and put Snowball in the fenced-in yard.

One day while my sister and I were playing in the front yard, we saw a piece of tin laying off to the side of our driveway. Snowball started to bark and growl at us, but we didn't know what made him so upset.

Our dad heard all the noise and came around to the front yard to see what was happening. Dad saw us on this piece of tin and yelled at us to stay put and not to move.

"Why?" we asked because that was what we were supposed to do, wasn't it? We were just kids.

"There's a snake under that piece of tin," he said softly so we wouldn't get too scared.

Dad came running up to us with a garden hoe to kill the snake. Snowball kept the snake busy while dad got behind it to kill it.

A few weeks later, Snowball was killed by a pack of wild dogs in the woods. Our older brother found him, and brought him home to be buried in the field beside the house.

My sister and I cried for a long time.

This showed me what a dog would do, if we loved him and took care of him.

We loved our dog, Snowball.

CHAPTER 8
IN SAMMY'S WORDS—BASEMENTS

When I was a teenager living on the south side of Columbus, Ohio, we lived in a two-story house right on the corner of Sixth and Reeb Avenue. This house had a basement, where my folks placed a pool table they bought for me for Christmas.

When you went down into our basement, there was an old staircase made of wood. The walls were rock and wood. There was no cement of any kind.

As you reached the bottom of the wooden staircase, on the right side of this wall was a hole just big enough for one person to crawl into. On the other side of the wall, it was very scary. No one would ever crawl into the hole to see what was there.

I guess you could say that hole and all those noises in it made everyone scared. You could say no one was brave enough to find out what was on the other side of that hole.

I remember one time the policemen were looking for my brother Dave, who had supposedly stolen a car.

Dave was going to crawl into that hole, but decided against it and gave himself up. He was afraid of what was on the other side of that hole.

Chapter 9
IN SAMMY'S WORDS—BAD SMELL

It was nighttime, and I was driving home with the windows down as I smelled the fresh country air. After a while I started to get sleepy, so I turned on the radio to try to stay awake. That didn't help; not this time anyway.

All of a sudden I got this whiff of a smell that made me think someone had died.

It was a skunk that someone or something had gotten too close to.

Now, that smell woke me up.

If you should happen to run over a skunk, the smell will stay in your car for weeks and you will have to wash your clothes several times.

I did.

CHAPTER 10
IN SAMMY'S WORDS—
SEEING CHILDHOOD FRIENDS

While walking down the street of my hometown, all of a sudden I saw an old friend I ran around with from when I was a child to a teenager. I didn't believe it was him at first. I didn't believe it was Robert Hunt.

I was so glad to see him because we used to go fishing, to the movies, and play baseball together. We even went out on double dates.

Robert saved my life one time, when we were swimming in a lake and I got cramps in my legs. I couldn't swim. Robert helped me back to shore.

The first thing I did when I saw Robert was give him a big hug and ask him what he had been doing. I wanted to know where he lived, was he married, and how many kids he had.

Then I started telling him about old times, and asked if he had seen any of our other friends. I wanted to know if he wanted to get together and have dinner.

It was so good to see him, even for such a short time.

CHAPTER 11
IN SAMMY'S WORDS—FAMILY FEUD

Annie and I were living in Columbus, Ohio on the north side of town in an apartment complex. We had a three-bedroom apartment, and the complex was for low-income families. Annie and I were in that bracket, because I had been hurt in a car accident and I wasn't able to work.

I had back surgery that was called a fusion. I was suing the person I had the accident with and was trying to get Social Security Disability.

Annie and I had three children, one girl and two boys.

One day after living there about six months, paying our rent and buying food with welfare and food stamps, my lawyer called and said they wanted to settle out of court. The insurance company was going to pay all of my hospital bills, and forty thousand dollars extra.

I took the deal.

That same month I was granted my Social Security Disability and back pay for one year from the day I signed up for SSI. I received ten thousand each for Annie and me. There was a second check for our kids. We put the money in the bank and went to

Welfare and gave them back that months check. I told them we were giving back the check, and getting off welfare for good.

Annie and I paid off our bills, and my mom and dad for all the help they gave us during the hard times. Annie took her sister out to do some shopping. I took my brother and cousin to do some shopping, too.

I got a job because my back was doing pretty good.

My cousin Tom and his wife Kate were at our house, and he told me how he hated his job and that his car was falling apart.

"I'll get you a job where I work," I told Tom.

I got him a job working from seven in the morning to three thirty in the afternoon.

"My car is junk, I need something to drive back and forth to work," said Tom.

I loaned him some money to get another car.

One day my boss wanted to know why Tom hadn't shown up for work. I had no answer, but I was going to find out, so I drove to Tom and Kate's house.

"That job is too hard, and I'm not going to go back to work anymore," Tom whined.

"How are you planning to pay me back the money you borrowed to buy your car?" I asked.

"Me and Kate ain't going to pay it back," he said.

He was right, he never paid me the money he borrowed.

CHAPTER 12
IN SAMMY'S WORDS—
THE STOLEN CARS

Ella's heart was telling her that Sammy's end of time was drawing near.

She encouraged him to write. She wanted him to continue to write about the part of his life in which Ella didn't participate.

This was how he began his story again:

***

I was fifteen and living in Columbus, Ohio on the corner of Smith and Rheam with my mom and dad. I attended Barrett Junior High School for two years, and then I went to South High School. I was doing pretty well in school. I had a lot of friends and did what normal teenagers do, like play sports and go to parties with my girl.

Where I lived, I had to walk a mile and a half to school and back home all winter long. There weren't any school buses in our area, so my friends and I would walk to school together.

Well, one day one of my friends came over to my house and asked if I wanted to go and meet some girls in a town called Ashland, Kentucky.

"Sure, but why do we have to travel that far to meet some girls? Don't we have enough girls here in Columbus?" I asked jokingly.

Tom was the friend who came to my house.

My name is Sammy.

"How many girls are there, and who is going with us?"

"You, me, and my two brothers, Jake and Eddy," said Tom.

I thought about it for a few seconds and said, "Yeah, I'll go. How are we planning to get there?"

"I'm going to borrow a car from a friend," answered Tom.

Around six that evening, Tom and his brothers pulled up in front of my house. I got in and we left, driving on Route 23 South to Ashland, Kentucky.

Tom was acting strange.

"What's wrong, Tom?" I asked.

He didn't answer me.

Jake and Eddy, his brothers, weren't saying a word.

Halfway down there to Ashland, we ran out of gas.

"Do you have any money for gas?" I asked Tom.

I had about fifteen dollars on me. Jake and Eddy had about five dollars each, but they weren't planning on buying any gas. Instead, Jake went into a driveway, broke into a car, and started pulling and twisting the wires under the steering column.

"What the hell are you doing?" I demanded.

Jake started the car and backed it up right into a deep ditch.

Well, everyone started to scatter.

I started walking back to Columbus while Tom, Jake, and Eddy started walking towards Ashland.

About fifteen minutes later, a state trooper pulled up behind me. The trooper got out of his car and walked up to me.

"Where are you headed?" he asked.

"I'm on my way home from my aunt's house. I've been walking for most of the day," I answered with a big lie.

"I've patrolled the road all day. I didn't see you walking until now."

"I didn't see you either," I answered a little too smart-alecky.

Another officer showed up in a vehicle that contained Tom, Jake, and Eddy flattened against the back seat.

The two officers talked to each other.

The first officer who talked to me walked over and told me, "You're under arrest for stealing two cars."

"What are you talking about?" I asked.

"Those boys in the back of that police car said that all of you stole a car in Columbus earlier in the evening."

We were taken to jail in Waverly, Ohio. That was the closest town, where we spent the night. The next morning two plain-clothes officers came from Columbus to take us to the Columbus jail, to stand trial for auto theft.

Tom and I were the two oldest boys, so we were sentenced to six months in the county work house. Jake and Eddy got probation.

After about three months in the work house, I decided to take off from there.

I got away okay. I went to Lockbourne, Ohio, to see my cousins.

My cousins were swimming in the local pond, close to town. I was talking with them and my girlfriend, Annie, when a town officer stopped beside us.

"You two girls need to go home," he said. He looked toward Annie and another girl.

"No," Annie said.

"No, you don't have to go. You're not doing anything wrong, Annie," I said to her.

"Shut your mouth," said the officer.

"Get lost," I snapped back.

The town cop got out of his car and started to chase my cousins and me. We went under a railroad bridge and up the other side to get to a road.

"Why are you running?" asked Steve and Fred, my two cousins.

"Because I escaped from the county jail," I shouted.

We ran up the hill to where the railroad tracks were, and there just happened to be train stopped there. I climbed under one of the railroad cars to hide.

All of a sudden the train started to move. My two cousins started to yell at me and tried to get the train to stop. That was not going to happen.

I was lucky because the train engine had already passed over where I was hiding. I just had to wait for the rest of the cars and caboose to move over my position where I was lying on the tracks.

"Boy, you are the luckiest person I ever knew," said Steve, as Fred nodded in agreement.

We went on our way to Steve and Fred's house to see if their mom, my Aunt Ethel, would take me to my other aunt's house. That would be my Aunt Mary, who lived on the bank of the Ohio River outside of Manchester, Ohio, on Route 52. Aunt Ethel took me to Aunt Mary's.

I was there for a few days.

One night my mother and father showed up at Aunt Mary's house.

"We're going to take you back to jail so you won't have to be on the run for the rest of your life," said my dad, Vern, as my mom, Teresa, stood next to him.

I looked at Aunt Mary.

"I called your mom and dad," she said, as she averted her eyes from my questioning glance.

I didn't get mad at her, because I knew she was doing what was best for me.

So, I went back to jail. They added two more months to my term, and two weeks in solitary confinement for escaping in the first place.

Before I knew it, my time passed and I was a free man.

I was glad to be home free, and not have to worry about the police chasing me.

About two weeks later my mom received a call from her niece, telling her Aunt Bessie was killed at Columbus Motor Speedway.

One of the race cars wrecked and lost its tire. The tire came flying over the fence and hit Aunt Bessie and mom's niece, Sandy. Sandy was going to have a baby in two months, but she lost it after the accident.

We all went to the funeral; some of my family didn't want to talk to me because I had just gotten out of jail.

I didn't care, because I was free man.

I did get to see my old girlfriend. Her name was Sally Nichols. We broke up because I was stupid and young, and didn't know that I had a good thing at the time.

What I was trying to say was that everyone gets into trouble, but it's best to pay your dues and not worry about looking over your shoulder for the rest of your life.

Chapter 13
IN SAMMY'S WORDS—UFOS

Sammy's life was not boring. Ella wished she had been a part of his youth and the fun she knew he'd had.

***

For as long as I can remember, I've been hearing about people who have seen UFOs (Unidentified Flying Objects) flying around in the sky.

I always thought those people were crazy and didn't know what they were talking about, until one evening while my cousin and I, along with our girlfriends, were sitting in the front yard of Annie's house. Annie was my girlfriend. The other friends with us were Denver, Brenda, Russ, and Sue. We were all talking about what we would do if we saw a UFO in the sky.

Annie's parents lived in the country, surrounded by woods and mountains. We were just sitting around and doing what teenagers do, and that's not a lot.

Russ was looking over into the woods when he said, "Hey, you guys, look over there. It's a UFO."

"Don't start that stuff, you know there's no such thing as a UFO," we said as we all talked in the general direction of where Russ was pointing.

"Look for yourself," said Russ as he continued to point.

We all turned to look and saw something that looked like a UFO; it had all kinds of lights around it. The lights were rotating in a circle.

"Let's go check out this UFO," one of the boys shouted.

We drove up one road and down another for about two or three hours. We were about to stop looking, because we couldn't find the right road to get us close to the lights, when we came upon a dirt road that looked like it went straight toward the brightness.

We headed up that road, and came upon a fence surrounding the land where the lights were shining. All we could see from where we were sitting in the car were some lights on the other side of the woods.

We were scared half to death, but we kept watching, trying to figure out if we should climb the fence and take a look-see or not.

Suddenly we were surrounded by bright, flashing lights from several police cars.

We didn't have any idea of what was happening.

The police officers demanded that we climb into the police cars and we were driven to the police station. The officers wanted to know what we were doing out there on that road, and why we were sitting on that fence.

"We were hunting down something that looked like a UFO," I said apprehensively.

The officers started laughing, and they all left the room where we were being held, for at least a half hour. We didn't know what to expect.

"You all can go home, but we need you to stop chasing UFOs," the officer said, when he returned to the room where we were waiting.

"Do you want to go back and check out the UFO?" asked Russ as we were leaving the police station.

"Not on your life," I answered. "Being taken to the police station once a night is plenty enough for me. What do you think?" I asked the two girls, who were nodding in agreement.

We never did find out if what we saw was a UFO.

We did find out what it felt like to be arrested, or almost arrested

We never did go looking for UFOs again.

CHAPTER 14
IN SAMMY'S WORDS—FIRST LOVE

It was hard to hear the one you love express his love for another woman, but Ella had asked him to do it. She'd asked him to write about his life.

***

One afternoon while playing basketball at our local school, Bob, Ken, and I decided to go home and then go to a movie. We all left the basketball court and went home, to take a shower and get all that sweat and stink off of us.

The movie we decided to see was playing at a local theater. The movie we were going to see was *Beach Blanket Bingo*. While we were sitting in our seats, three nice-looking girls came in. They seated themselves on the other side of the movie theater.

"Sammy, I dare you to go over there and say hi to them," said Bob and Ken as they glanced at the girls.

Well, I did it.

A few minutes passed and I said, "Hello, Girls."

They turned around, smiled, and said "Hi, back at you."

Bob and Ken came over and joined me.

50

The girl I was talking to was Annie. Her two sisters were Betsy and Brenda.

"Annie, can I come over here and sit beside you?" I asked shyly.

"No, I'll come back there and sit next to you," she replied.

When that happened, Ken sat beside Betsy and Bob sat next to Brenda.

Annie and I started talking, and we asked each other what school we attended.

Bob, Ken, and I went to South High School. Annie, Betsy, and Brenda went to Hamilton High School further down the road, close to Lockbourne, Ohio. That's where Annie said she lived.

"How old are you, Annie?" I asked.

"Sixteen."

Annie and I didn't get to see much of the movie, because we were making out in the darkness of the movie theater. Before we knew it, the movie was over and Annie had to get ready to leave.

Her dad was outside, waiting for the girls to exit the movie theater. Before she left, I got her phone number and gave her mine.

About a week later, I called Annie. We couldn't call any sooner, because we both had to go to school and do some homework.

Bob, Ken, and I called each of the sisters and asked if they wanted to go to a movie. They all said yes. I had a '55 Chevy, and told the girls that we would pick them up.

When Bob, Ken, and I picked up the girls, I said to Annie, "You look real nice. I sure am glad you let me see you again."

The following week I called Annie again, but she never answered the phone. Annie's mother answered the phone.

"May I talk to Annie?" I asked her mother.

"No, she's not here. She's in a girls' home for troubled girls," explained Annie's mom.

"What is she doing there?" I asked angrily.

"She got into a fight at school with her sisters. They were beating on her pretty bad."

I had no idea Annie and her two sisters would do that. Annie had two other sisters besides Brenda and Betsy. They were Mary and Ella. She also had two brothers, Jimmy and Tom.

Bob, Ken, and I never got to talk to the girls for three weeks.

"Can we come by to see you girls? Bob and Ken will come with me. Is that all right?" I asked, hoping the girls would agree.

"Sure," Annie replied. "I would like that, Sammy. I'm sure my sisters would, too."

"What time do you want us to be there?"

"Four o'clock."

The three of us arrived at Annie's house at 3:45 PM. All six of us decided to just walk around the town of Lockbourne.

Annie and I were having a nice walk by ourselves. Then the other two couples joined us, and we saw a church lot filled with parked cars.

"Let's go to church," said Annie. "I think we all need a little help."

I agreed with her, gladly.

The preacher was giving the sermon when he suddenly stopped talking and looked over our heads. The preacher looked really mad.

Ken, Betsy, Annie, and I turned around to see what was wrong. There were Bob and Brenda, making out in the back row of the church.

The preacher came to where we were sitting and said, "Leave, now. I want you out of here."

We all left the church.

"What are we going to do now?" chimed in Bob, Ken, Betsy, and Brenda.

"We're going to walk around some more," I said.

"We don't want to walk any more," said the two other couples, leaving Annie and me to walk alone.

Annie and I found a place to sit down and talk, and, of course, to kiss. We sat at the top of some steps in front of an old building in the center of Lockbourne, Ohio.

Everything was going okay until Bob, Ken, and the girls came to where we were sitting.

"Get in the car," said Bob.

"We have to go," added Ken.

"What for?" I asked.

"Ken smarted off to one of the local boys," answered Bob.

"What did you say to make these boys mad enough to fight or beat us up?" I demanded.

"I called the boy a redneck country boy," replied Ken.

We climbed into the car and dropped off the girls at their home.

There were three carloads of local boys coming after us. Bob stepped on the gas, and was doing sixty-five. We drove to an intersection where we had to make a hard right or a hard left. Bob took a hard right on two wheels, and I thought we were done for, but we made it. We went home.

The telephone was ringing when I got inside the house.

"Sammy?"

"Hi, Annie," I said

"Are you all right?" Annie asked

"Yeah, sure. I'm fine."

"I saw those cars chasing you guys. I was really worried. I guess you won't be coming back to see me, will you?"

"Why would you say that?" I asked.

"There might be more trouble," she said.

"I'll be there in a couple of days."

"Really?"

Annie and I kept seeing each other for a year, and then we decided to get married because Annie was going to have my baby daughter.

"Sammy, my mom said she is going to make me get rid of the baby," cried Annie as I held her close to me.

"I won't let her do that, if that's not what you want to do," I whispered softly to Annie.

"I want our baby," she cried softly.

"Don't worry, Annie. I'll take care of everything."

Annie was almost smiling when I took her home that evening.

"Get some clothes together, Annie, and I will be there to pick you up. We're going to Tennessee," I said excitedly. "Don't tell anyone where we're going, promise me."

"All right."

No one knew what we were going to do. We took off and went to Dyersburg, Tennessee, where we got an apartment for forty-five dollars a month rent.

I found a job working for the City of Dyersburg.

Annie called her sister about a month later, to see what was going on at home.

"Mom and dad are looking all over the place for you guys," said Betsy. "Sammy's mom is doing the same thing."

A month later Annie had our baby girl. We named her Mindy Dawn.

We started attending church regularly. When Preacher Norman Folks found out that we weren't married, he convinced us to do it. We wanted to get married anyway, not just because he said we should do it.

We lived in Dyersburg, Tennessee, for about two years. In that time Annie had our second child, a baby boy, whom we named Nelson Dwayne.

My job was picking up trash. While working one day for the city, we had to go by my place and my little girl saw me. She started crawling to me. My heart was so full of love for that little girl.

Preacher Norman came by that night and told me about a better job working in a factory.

The factory made those foam pads that go under rugs.

I got the job, and worked there for almost a year until one day, this big roll of foam came off the conveyer belt and landed on top of me. My coworkers tried to get that big rubber mat off me, but the roll weighed over four hundred pounds. The emergency medical technicians said they thought I had a broken neck.

I was taken to the local hospital. The doctor there said I needed to be transferred to Memphis, Tennessee, where there were better doctors.

The hospital transferred me to Memphis in the back of a hearse.

I didn't like that very much. While I was riding in back of that hearse, I thought about all those other people who were supposed to be on their way to the funeral home. Was that where I was headed?

The curtains were open at the back of the hearse. When a car would pull up beside the hearse, people would look in the back to see if the person was male or female, and if they were young or old. When the person riding in the back all of a sudden started to raise his head up and look back, the carload of looking people would almost have an accident, because it would scare the devil out them. Bodies in a hearse weren't supposed to rise up and look back at them.

We finally arrived at the hospital, and I was rolled into the hallway to wait to see a doctor.

Several hours passed, and still no doctor.

I sat up on the cot and started moving around.

I crawled off the stretcher and was trying to leave, or something, when one of the new doctors coming on duty saw me and asked the other staff members what I was doing there, walking around the emergency room hall. Because I had a neck brace on, I was having a hard time getting around.

When one of the nurses said that I was there from Dyersburg, Tennessee, with neck and back injuries, they put me back on the stretcher and started working on me right away.

The doctor gave me a shot, and I went to sleep.

The next thing I remember was that I was in a room upstairs. Two days had passed. The nurse said I could call my home in Dyersburg to let my wife know I was doing okay.

Annie couldn't make it down to the hospital, because she didn't know the way to Memphis, Tennessee. I was so disappointed.

One evening she showed up in my room.

Annie had gotten to the hospital because she called her mom and dad, who drove her to see me. Annie also called my mom and dad. So Annie, Mindy, Nelson, her mom and dad, and my mother were all in my room.

While they were there, the doctor showed up to check me out.

"Can I go home, Doctor John?"

"Yes, you can," he said. He exited the room to write out the release orders and prescriptions that I needed to retrieve from the pharmacy before leaving.

We were home for a few days when Annie asked me, "Would you like to go back home, to stay where our families live?"

"Okay," I said, with apprehension.

My parents and Annie's parents never got along, because each blamed the other for our running away together.

Annie and I told both sets of parents that we were married, and that was that.

A few months passed. Annie and I had our own place, and I was back working at a gas station.

One evening while I was pumping gas, Annie's mom called our house crying. She said they'd found Annie's dad, dead in his car at work.

He had committed suicide. He had put a hose on his muffler and into his car window. No one knew why he killed himself.

A few months later, Annie received another phone call. It was Annie's mom again, and she was crying.

"What's wrong now, Mom?' Annie asked, dreading the explanation for the tears.

"They found your brother dead in his car. He committed suicide."

Annie knew her brother couldn't stand not having his dad around, but she didn't dream he would kill himself.

Things settled down and Annie and I were doing okay. Her sisters would come over to stay a few days or weekend. My cousins Buck and Raymond would visit, also.

Annie and I were very happy, and everything was doing fine because our families had finally learned to get along.

CHAPTER 15
IN SAMMY'S WORDS— DEADLY SHOOTING

Sammy got to see a lot that did not include Ella.

***

I entered the army in 1969 to get some kind of training, like driving a truck or operating a front-end loader, something to make things better for my family. I got that training, but I also learned how to be a very good rifle shooter. They were training us to get ready to go to Vietnam. I never got to go to Vietnam because I was an only child, and they wouldn't send me over there.

I did have to go to Germany, where I spent eighteen months.

While I was overseas, I got to come home on a thirty-day leave. Boy, was I glad to come home, because I never got to see or talk to my wife, Annie. I didn't tell her I was coming home for thirty days because I wanted to surprise her.

I did just that. When she came to the door to see who was knocking, I put my finger over the peephole so she couldn't see who was standing on the other side of the door. When I took my hand off the peephole so she could see who was standing there, she yanked the door open. I thought she was going to pull my head off trying to get me inside of the apartment. We lived on Cherry Street, on the west side of Columbus, Ohio.

After being home for about fifteen days, my cousin Bobby and his wife came over to visit us. Bobby, his brother Eddy, and I grew up together. We went to the same school, on the same side of town. We were all good friends and did everything together.

While he was at our house, he asked Annie and me to come over to his house to play some cards and just hang out.

Bobby had a little boy about the same age as my son Beau.

We went over to his house, on the north side of town. When we got there, his younger brother Adam was there. Bobby and I were teammates, and Annie and Sandy were teammates. Sandy was Bobby's wife.

We were playing Euchre. Everything was going okay, until they started to drink gin.

Bobby and Sandy got into fight, because Sandy was getting drunk and loud. Annie and I weren't drinking because Annie never did like any kind of liquor.

Sandy got mad at Bobby because Bobby poured the fifth of gin down the kitchen sink. Sandy called Bobby every name she could think of except a white man. Sandy ran out of the house, and went two doors down from where they lived.

I don't know what happened to Bobby, because he just went off the deep end. He started to run around the house, pushing everyone out of his way.

"Bobby, what are you doing? Stop it right now!" I said. I tried to stop him and settle him down, but I couldn't get the job done. Bobby ran upstairs to his mother's bedroom and pulled out a sawed-off, twenty-two rifle, and checked to see if it was loaded.

It was loaded.

Bobby ran back downstairs to the front room where my daughter, my wife, and three sons, plus Adam were waiting. Bobby's infant son and my infant son were lying on the daybed, right beside the front door. Bobby ran over to the fireplace, and I got in front of him to try and stop him from whatever he was planning to do.

"Don't be stupid, Bobby!" I yelled at him.

Bobby put the gun to my chest and said, "Get back, or I will shoot you."

I froze. I didn't know what to do, so I backed off in hopes he would calm down. Bobby went to where the daybed was and pointed the gun at his three-month-old baby boy. My son was the same age. I was so worried that he would shoot my son. I couldn't go for the gun because of my son's sleeping body being one foot from his sleeping son. Bobby stood there for what seemed like forever, looking down at his son and mine.

Bobby held the gun right on his son's forehead, right between his son's eyes. His son was asleep, and had no idea what was going to happen.

There wasn't a sound to be heard. Then came the sound of a gun going off.

Bobby threw the gun out of the front room window. The two boys were covered with glass, but his son also had a bullet hole right between his eyes.

Bobby said, "Help me, Sammy."

"There's nothing I can do for you," I said as I held a white rag over the baby's wound to stop the bleeding.

The bullet went through the baby's head, through the two mattresses, through the floor, and into the basement.

"Annie, call 9-1-1 and get some help here."

In minutes the police were there.

They came running into the house. One officer picked up baby Jake in his arms and headed to the front door, while the other officer put handcuffs on Bobby. The police officers took Bobby and left the room. By the time the officers reached the hospital, baby Jake was dead. The doctors told the two police officers that there wasn't anything that could be done to save baby Jake.

Some other detectives came and took Annie and me to the police station, to take our statement of what happened. When we arrived at the police station Bobby was already there, sitting in a holding cell. They brought Bobby to where we were sitting. Bobby still had that blank look on his face. He never did say why he killed baby Jake.

After the detectives took our statements, they said we would have to go to the trial in a couple of weeks. I told the detectives I couldn't wait for the trial, because I had to report back to my unit in Mannheim, Germany.

After I reported back to my unit, while I was still in Germany, we got orders to get ready for some war games. We had to travel to Bombholder, Germany, for these war games. About a week into the war games, we were in the field on a hillside alongside some tanks; there were some tanks on top of the hillside right in front of us, too. All of a sudden one of the tanks started rolling back down the hill, straight at us.

The tank lost its brakes. It looked like it was heading straight at us. Our captain got scared because the tank was going to hit us. He jumped off the personnel carrier. When he landed on the ground, he hurt his leg and couldn't move. The tank missed us, but ran over the captain. He was smashed flat and died instantly.

They stopped the war games and let everyone go back to base. There was a big funeral for the captain.

While I was at the graveyard, I thought about why everyone was dying in front of me.

We went back to Mannheim, Germany, and we were sitting around the barracks cleaning our weapons. After I got my weapon cleaned I took it back to the weapon station. While I was standing there, another serviceman came in carrying a fifty-caliber machine gun on his shoulder. He was planning to put the fifty-caliber on the counter, but his hands slipped and it fell down on my foot.

My foot was broken.

I went to the infirmary, where they put a cast on my foot.

This broken foot happened with about three months left on my tour of duty before I would get to go home.

A month before my getting out, they told me I wouldn't be able to go home with that cast on my foot. They told me they don't let people on an airplane with a cast on any part of their body. So I told the doctor to take the cast off, because I was going home.

While I was overseas for eighteen months, they kept Bobby in jail waiting for me to come home. I was home on leave in 1970. I was released from the army in 1971.

About two weeks after my arriving home, they said they were going to start the trial.

My wife Annie and I had to testify about what had happened. The jury found my cousin Bobby guilty, and sentenced him to twenty-five years in prison.

Annie and I visited Bobby and talked to him.

In Bobby's mind, he never did anything and shouldn't be in jail.

This showed me what drinking could do to someone.

The worst thing about all of this was that baby Jake was just sleeping and being a good little boy.

Chapter 16
IN SAMMY'S WORDS—
THE DROWNING OF TWO BOYS

Sammy's life continues:

***

About two months after my leaving the Army, Annie and I decided to take the kids to the fairgrounds and see a wrestling match. The fairgrounds were about five miles away from my home, on the north side of town. We didn't mind making that walk, because it was a beautiful day. The sun was bright and there was a gentle breeze.

On the way to the fairgrounds, about two blocks from our home, there was a river and a waterfall. Annie and I, along with the kids, were getting close to the bridge where it crossed the river to downtown, when a man came running up to us. The man was elderly and he was having a hard time breathing.

"Run for help!" shouted the elderly man.

"Why? What's wrong?" I asked.

"Two boys fell into the river near the waterfall."

I turned around and started to run back to a little store so I could use their telephone, when I looked up and there was a police vehicle coming down the street. I waved my arms and hands while standing in the middle of the street.

"What's the problem here?" asked the police officer, after pulling over to the side of the street.

"Two boys fell into the river where the waterfall is!" I shouted.

One of the officers got out the police vehicle and ran to the riverbank. I was standing right beside him.

The officer took off his belt, which held his gun and hand-cuffs. The other officer called his dispatcher, saying they needed help because two young boys fell into the river.

The fire department, an ambulance, and some other police cars started arriving at the scene.

"Do you see them?" asked the officer standing beside me.

"No," I replied sadly.

Annie and I gathered the kids together and went on our way to the fairgrounds. We were wondering if they ever found the boys while we were sitting at the wrestling match.

We all arrived home at around ten o'clock that evening. Annie and I put the kids to bed, and went into the front room to watch television. We waited for the news. At eleven o'clock on the local news, the first thing they talked about was those two boys who drowned. They were eight and nine years old.

"The two boys were found two miles down the river, and both were dead," stated the reporter.

Our kids weren't allowed to even think about going close to that river.

***

About a month and a half later, Annie asked, "Sammy, will you teach me how to drive a car?"

"Yes, I sure will. You need to know how to drive a car in case something should happen to me."

For the next month, I was out teaching Annie how to drive a car. It had to have an automatic transmission, because you never want to teach someone to drive with a standard. There was too much to think about, and too much coordination for a beginner.

I had her ready to take the written test and the driving test. Annie passed both with flying colors.

A few weeks after getting her license, Annie wanted to get away and go to the mall.

"Sure, go ahead," I said as Annie and her best friend climbed into the car.

There were gone for about four hours when the telephone rang.

"Sammy, the car won't start," Annie said.

"Will it turn over or try to start?" I probed.

"No," was her reply.

I found a babysitter, Annie's sister Brenda, to watch the kids. I boarded a transit bus that took me to the mall where she was stranded.

I looked at the car, checking the battery and everything else I could think of that could be the problem. Then I looked at the gear shift; the car was in drive. I looked at Annie and started to laugh.

"What's so funny?" she demanded.

"You called me to come all the way over here to the mall to put this car in park and start the car. Annie, you have the gear shift in drive. The car won't start while positioned in that gear," I said, as I tried to control my laughter.

I started the car and she drove us home, but I was laughing so hard I was hurting.

Annie turned to me and punched me hard to get my attention, and to stop me from laughing.

"If you say anything to anyone, I'll break both of your arms," she said angrily.

"I won't say a word because this can happen to anybody," I said as I continued to struggle with the laughter.

CHAPTER 17
IN SAMMY'S WORDS—
THE HAUNTED TRAILER

We lived in a mobile home on a one-lane dirt road on the outskirts of Plain Town, Ohio. My sister, Betsy, lived on the same road about a mile from us. At night this road was pitch black, and surrounded by woods on both sides.

We loved living there. I had a job working in a sawmill. The sawmill shut down because of lack of business, so I went to Columbus one day, along with Annie, to find a job. While I was looking for work, Annie stayed with another one of her sisters.

I found a job that day driving a truck, so Annie and I had to move to Columbus because I needed to be close to my job. We found an apartment on the north side of Columbus.

My sister's son, Mark, told everyone who came to see his mom that his trailer was haunted. Mark would say he would see his dad walking down the hallway every night. Mark's father killed himself in that trailer a year earlier.

One day my sister called our house. She wanted to come up to visit with us for a couple of weeks. Of course we said okay.

About a week after they got there, Josh, my brother-in-law, wanted to take a trip to the trailer to see if everything was okay. Josh asked me to go with him.

I had this friend called BJ, a tall black man who was as nice a man you would ever want to meet. BJ and his wife, Liz, lived next door to us in the apartment complex.

BJ and I would get together and play chess. BJ was a lot better at it than I was, but that didn't matter to me. Sometimes BJ, Liz, Annie, and I would play card games while the kids played together upstairs in their rooms. We all got along really well.

I asked BJ to go along with us, because he had never been to that part of the country and he wanted to see what it was like, as well as see the scenery.

Josh, BJ, and I left early in the afternoon so BJ could see the countryside. The trip took almost three hours to get to Plain Town. It was another fifteen minutes to find the trailer.

When we arrived at the trailer, it was pitch black and located on a one-lane road. We pulled into the driveway, and it was so dark we couldn't see the trailer without our headlights shining.

Josh was the first one out of the car. He entered first and turned the power on so we could check the trailer.

BJ and I went into the trailer next. We couldn't see a thing, but we heard Josh down the hall, where the power box was located.

All of a sudden Josh started screaming and running like he had a tiger on his tail.

BJ turned as white as I ever saw a black man turn, when he was scared.

"Run, my dad is after us!" Josh yelled.

"So what?" BJ said.

"My dad is dead," screamed Josh.

BJ turned around and knocked me on my butt to the floor. Josh ran over me to the door. BJ and Josh were already in the car with the engine running when I climbed into the passenger side. BJ stepped on the gas, and we went flying down the dirt road.

Josh and I were laughing so hard we didn't know whether or not BJ knew where he was going.

After driving about two miles down the road, BJ stopped the car and said, "What the hell are you two laughing about?"

"There really wasn't any ghost, BJ," Josh and I said.

"Then what was that all about?" asked BJ.

"Josh and I wanted to play a joke on you and see what you would do," I said.

I thought BJ was going to kill both of us, he was so mad.

Then BJ started laughing with us.

"I'll pay you two back for this," he said with a smile.

We went back to the trailer, and Josh turned on the lights on so we could check it out. We arrived back in Columbus at about eleven that night.

I smiled every time I thought about the fun we had that night.

The smile turned to a frown when I remembered the night I was told that BJ was shot and killed. I sure did miss him.

CHAPTER 18
IN SAMMY'S WORDS—CPR CLASS

When I took a CPR (Cardiopulmonary Resuscitation) class, I learned how much my hands meant to me. When I used my hands to do chest compressions on a person using CPR, if I did it right, I could save that person's life. If I used my hands the wrong way, I could do more damage than good.

I had to do CPR on a person to know how it felt to save a life.

Doing CPR on kids and infants was a very delicate thing. On an infant one month to three years old, I used just two fingers and one small breath. If I used my two fingers to do CPR on an infant and kids, when he or she came back to life, I knew how important my hands were.

I loved the idea that I could help someone with my very own hands.

CHAPTER 19
IN SAMMY'S WORDS— HEART PROBLEMS

You might be in the best of health and be at work, just sitting watching television, walking around to lose weight, or you might even be driving a car, when all of a sudden, your chest would be hurting and you were having a hard time breathing. You sat down somewhere and thought it was just heartburn.

While you were sitting there, you started to feel better. Then you went home, because your chest had stopped hurting. You didn't think any more about it.

These were some of the signs of a heart attack, and they would fool you.

The first ten minutes after the pains hit could put the person between life and death. The first thing you needed to do was call 9-1-1, and get help to come to your house. You could start CPR and help the family member back to life. Most EMS (Emergency Medical Service) workers would continue CPR and get an IV started. Then you could hear the EMS worker say we have to load and go, and get your family member to the emergency room.

I didn't know I had that bad of a heart problem. I knew I had a few problems, but not enough to cause a heart attack. In 1994 I had my first heart attack, in the last week of November.

I was getting ready to take my wife, Ella, to work. I was pouring some coffee into my wife's thermos bottle when all of a sudden, I couldn't breathe. My wife came out of the bathroom because she heard me gasping for air.

Ella helped me to the couch, where I lay down. She called 9-1-1 and had Golden Star Ambulance come to our house to get me to the hospital. I knew I was in trouble when the ambulance arrived at our house.

The EMS person came into the house and put an oxygen level monitor on my finger. Donnie Turner told the other EMT to get the oxygen tank and a non-rebreather mask for me, so I could breathe better. They brought the stretcher in and put me on it. We went to the hospital, which was about two miles from our house. After arriving at the hospital in the ER, they started another IV for medication and called my heart doctor.

From 1994 to July of 2008, I've had open heart surgeries consisting of a triple by-pass and twenty-six stents. I have died three times and suffered with congestive heart failure twice. I have had a total of four heart attacks.

CHAPTER 20
EXTRAORDINARY MEASURES

As the boot flew across the room, she managed to duck so it wouldn't hit her on the side of the head.

"Sammy, watch what you're doing!" Ella shouted to get his attention. "What are you looking for?"

"Uh, some change. I dropped some change into the bottom of the closet," he answered, blushing because he'd been caught ransacking the closet.

"Change? How much change? If you need change, there's some in my handbag," Ella said kindly.

"It's a couple of the state quarters. I finally found a couple of the ones I was missing from my collection," he explained without looking at her.

"Do you want any help looking?" Ella asked.

"No, no, I'll find them, and I'll put everything back neatly. You just go on to work. I'll find them. They have to be in here somewhere," he said, as he continued to pilfer through the closet.

Ella didn't think anything more about the quarter search. He must have left the change in his trouser pocket. Then when he hung the pants in the closet, the change dropped to the floor. That was usually how it worked. He might have to look in every shoe and prowl to the bottom of each box, but she was sure he would find his missing change.

She just didn't want him to worry about it too much. Ella didn't want him to get his heart acting up again. Worry did that to him. It seemed to put a lot of unwanted pressure on an already weakened muscle.

A couple of hours after Ella arrived at work, she called Sammy. He had usually called her by nine o'clock, but she hadn't heard from him.

"God, I hope he's okay," Ella whispered.

The telephone rang and rang. She was ready to hang up the receiver and head for home when he answered.

"Hello," he said almost inaudibly.

"Sammy?"

"Ella, hi," he said as he tried to control his rapid breathing.

"What's wrong, Sammy?" she asked, as worry consumed her once again.

"Nothing."

"You don't sound good, Sammy. You sound a little congested. Tell me the truth," Ella demanded. "Are you feeling all right? Should I come home?"

"No, Ella, I'm fine. I am a little congested, but it will go away. I had to run in here to answer the phone. That's why I'm out of breath. I was outside looking around on the ground, to see if I lost my quarters out there."

"Which quarters are you looking for? I'll try to get them at the bank," she said in exasperation.

"No, I'll find mine. When you get home, I'll go through the car with a fine-toothed comb. They're around here somewhere."

Ella couldn't imagine why a couple of quarters were so important to him.

"Why didn't you call me? You normally call me, I don't have to call you. You know how much I worry about you being there alone. Why didn't you call? Please don't make me worry so much," said Ella, firmly.

"I was busy looking for the quarters. The time slipped up on me, that's all," Sammy answered.

"All right. You probably need to rest, Sammy. Go take a nap. Worry about the quarters another time," Ella said in calmer tone.

"Sure, Ella, okay," he answered half-heartedly.

"Call me when you wake up. Love you—bye," Ella said as she placed the receiver on its cradle.

His mad search for quarters didn't make sense to her. What was wrong with him?

Two hours passed and no telephone call from Sammy. Did he take his nap? Was he still asleep? Should she call him?

"No, no, he's not a baby," Ella told herself. "Don't treat him like one."

Ella waited.

Another hour passed and no telephone call from Sammy. She wanted to pick up that phone and dial it as quickly as possible.

"Stop it, Ella," she scolded. "He will call."

Finally the telephone rang, and Ella could see Sammy's name displayed across the caller ID.

"Sammy?"

"Ella, my chest hurts."

"Is it bad?"

"Yes."

"I'm going to hang up. I want you to dial 9-1-1 as soon as I hang up. I'm on my way out the door now. Can you dial 9-1-1?" Ella asked worriedly.

"Yes, I think so."

Ella turned off her computer without following the proper protocol and raced down the steps from the second floor.

"Jen, I've got to leave. Sammy is sick," Ella said, as she raced past the receptionist, who was sitting at her desk in the lobby.

The ten-minute trip to the house seemed to take a lifetime.

The ambulance was only a block away from the house, in the small shopping center that could be seen out her front door.

She arrived at home before the ambulance. She was upset that it took them so long to drive around the block.

Ella didn't want anyone to remind her that it takes a while to gather the team and climb aboard the vehicle, because she could see the stupid thing from her front door.

She ran inside the house. Sammy was gasping for breath as he sat in his recliner.

"They're here, Sammy. Keep hanging on," she pleaded. She held the front door open to allow the gurney to be rolled into the house.

"What's the problem?" asked the young paramedic.

"Heart," whispered Sammy. "I can't breathe, and it hurts."

The paramedic wound the plastic nasal tube around Sammy's head, hooking it under his nose, allowing the life-sustaining oxygen to help him breathe a little easier.

The second ambulance attendant wrapped his arm with a blood-pressure cuff and noticeably flinched when he wrote the high numbers onto his paper.

They did not tarry long, making Sammy ready for the short trip to the hospital, which was about a mile away from the house.

If Ella had known it would take them as long as it did to go around the block, she wouldn't have told Sammy to call them. She would have driven him herself. Ella could get him to the emergency room faster than they could.

They asked Sammy to walk to the gurney so they could strap him in and load him into the back of the ambulance.

She grabbed his medications, made sure the dog and cats were where they were supposed to be, locked the front door, and reached the hospital before they actually unloaded him.

Ella could tell the "a little congested" feeling had progressed to a major congestion problem. Fluid was coming out of this nose and mouth and any other orifice it could use to escape from his body.

The emergency room personnel rapidly pulled the curtains and worked fiercely, trying to save Sammy from the depths of death.

Ella stood across from the closed curtains so she would not be in the way of those working with Sammy.

"Mrs. Holcombe, does your husband have a living will?" asked the white-haired doctor.

"What do you mean?"

"Does he want us to take extraordinary measures to keep him alive?"

"Of course he wants you to do what you can. So do I," Ella said harshly, as the doctor walked through the curtains.

She could not believe they were asking her such a stupid question.

The work continued at a rapid pace.

A nurse appeared before Ella. "Does your husband have any other family you need to notify? If he does, I think you should do that soon, very soon."

"All of his family is in Ohio, except me and my two sons. I don't need to tell them anything because Sammy will get better," Ella said belligerently.

"Mrs. Holcombe, we are sending him to Roanoke. His doctor says he wants him there. A helicopter will be here soon," said the nurse in firm but consoling tone.

Ella said a silent prayer of thank you to God, and left the hospital to grab some clothes for a stay of at least three days. If she needed more, she would have to drive back home to get them.

A couple of days after arriving in Roanoke, being cared for by people who knew his medical problems best, he was well enough to talk to Ella sensibly.

"Ella, I wasn't looking for quarters," he said sheepishly.

"What were you looking for?" Ella asked.

"My wedding band. I can't find it anywhere. When I get out of here in a couple of days, I'll keep looking for it," he said, tears seeping into the corners of his eyes.

"Don't worry about the ring, Sammy. I still love you with or without that ring," Ella said softly.

"I love you, too, Ella."

CHAPTER 21
THE DECISION

Ella's husband was hanging on to life only because he was connected to a machine that was breathing for him. She didn't know how long they, the medical persons who supposedly knew much more than she did, were going to allow the machine to perform its function of keeping her husband alive before they made her decide what step she wanted to take next. It was not really a question of something she wanted. It was something she had to do, like it or not.

Ella's life went on, whether Sammy was sick or not. She wanted to spend day and night with him, but she couldn't.

He didn't know whether or not she was there because he was so deeply comatose, but just in case, Ella talked to him. She touched him, and let him know that she loved him.

It was Saturday, and Ella had driven for two hours from the home Sammy and she shared in Stillwell, Virginia, to the Veterans Hospital in a neighboring state.

"Hi, Baby," Ella said. She donned a yellow isolation gown and forced her short, stubby fingers into the rubber gloves she pulled from a box atop the metal rolling cabinet outside his pressurized, intensive care room, number twenty-eight.

"I can't stay long, Sammy," Ella rambled. "I've got to go to my book signing. It was too late to change it to a later date. I'm sort of obligated. I know you understand, but I'm sure I will be condemned by those who think they know better."

He was lying there with hoses attached everywhere imaginable. His face was relaxed. His eyes were closed. The machine was whispering with its breath of life.

He was in far better condition now than he was two days ago; not that he ever woke up, because he didn't. Two days ago he was having seizures. His eyes would fly open wide, and his arms would rise and fall with a loud thump.

"God," Ella prayed, "Tell me what I should pray for. Tell me whether I want him to live or to die. He wouldn't want to be a vegetable. That's not a life." The tears were welling, but she didn't want to cry. She didn't want Sammy to see the tears or hear from her scratchy voice that she was that scared.

The eye openings and thumps were occurring about every sixty seconds and the medical personnel were scurrying around searching for a way to put a halt to the seizure-provoked activity.

Sedation was prescribed, along with anti-seizure medication. Finally, the thumps slowed and disappeared, but so did all of the hope that he would wake up and see her, talk to her, or just breathe on his own.

Four doctors suddenly appeared at the doorway. That was a good thing. Ella was hoping to get an answer or two. Of course this was a teaching hospital, so three of the young men standing around gazing at her husband were doctors in training. The fourth person, a lady, was the teacher, and the one from whom she should get some answers.

"How long do you think he's going to stay like this?" Ella asked the doctor, knowing she wouldn't give a direct answer, at least not at first.

"Have you spoken with the neurologist?" the doctor asked.

"Yes," Ella answered as she began to regurgitate the information garnered from him. "He told me my husband has significant brain damage."

As she stood in front of Ella, the doctor's face transformed from a rushed, busy doctor's to a person's professing to care about Ella and how she felt.

"We are here for you as well as your husband. Especially for you, because you are alone with no family to support you," consoled the doctor.

Those words were really beginning to bother Ella. She was hearing them way too often, and they were sounding phonier every time; just like the gentle little pats on the back she was receiving from almost every medical person who entered the room.

"You can't keep him in ICU forever. How do you determine when to move him out of here?" Ella asked.

"You will have to make a decision once your husband has been off sedation for four or five days, and still showing no signs of climbing out of the coma," said the doctor.

Ella had heard a conversation earlier that told her thirty-six hours without sedation had passed. The time for decision making was getting nearer.

"You will need to decide if you want him attached to the respirator with a tracheotomy, allowing him to rest just as he is indefinitely, or if you want everything detached, allowing him to slip away gently," said the doctor.

Ella nodded her head in understanding. She couldn't speak. The words weren't there. The voice was completely gone.

Thirty-six hours had passed. Another forty-eight to seventy-two hours would need to pass before she would be backed into the black hole of choosing life or death for her husband.

In the meantime, she was going to her book signing. She was going to try to think good thoughts. She didn't want to dwell on the decision.

"Hey, Sammy, I've got to go. I love you," Ella said as she stripped away the gloves and gown.

The book signing was about a half hour drive from the hospital, but within the same metropolitan area.

It was too late to cancel the event when Sammy became so ill, because it had already been advertised locally, and it was scheduled more than six months prior to the actual book signing.

It was difficult to steer her thoughts away from Sammy, but the hospital staff assured her they would call her if there was any change in his condition.

Ella smiled and tried to convince people who were within earshot that her books were good and that they really needed to read them.

Her cellphone rang once, later in the afternoon. No one was at the other end and the caller was identified as "Unknown." Ella was glad that they were not able to reach her, at the time. She found out when she arrived back at the hospital after the book signing that they'd wanted the decision about pulling the tubes when her phone rang.

Ella continued to try to smile and sell her books, knowing what was waiting for her at the hospital.

The decision never left her thoughts, but it had already been made in her mind.

He would want to slip away peacefully, so that was what Ella would let him do.

"Just remember, Sammy, I love you with all my heart," Ella whispered before she stepped out of his room for the final time.

CHAPTER 22
THEN ELLA WAS ALONE

Ella stood next to his bed and waited for his chest to rise and fall with each intake of air. The male nurse was busy straightening hoses and blankets, paying no attention to his patient.

"He stopped breathing," Ella whispered sadly.

"What! He can't do that," said the flustered nurse.

The nurse stopped fussing with the equipment and immediately tried to prove she was wrong.

He pressed the call button and said in a controlled tone, "Tell the RN for 110 to come to the room now. It's urgent."

Ella calmly stood by and watched the male nurse grow increasingly impatient with what was happening. Her guess was that this was the first time he had experienced such a quick death on his watch.

The RN entered the room. As she looked at Ella, she barked instructions to the male nurse.

"Disconnect everything."

"He just got here. I hadn't finished..." said the flustered male nurse.

"That's okay, John. This was expected," the RN said.

Ella moved to a corner of the room, trying to force herself to disappear so she wouldn't be a part of the bad scene playing out before her.

"Ma'am, I'll get you a chair. Are you all right?" the RN asked Ella, forcing the hint of concern into her voice.

Ella was all right, physically. She was totally destroyed, mentally.

She nodded her head in response to RN's question.

Yes, Ella needed a chair to sit on before her rubbery legs decided they weren't going to hold her up any longer. Yes, she's okay, Ella thought.

Suddenly her reason for being in this Veterans Administration Hospital was no longer living. All she wanted to do was leave. All she was able to do was sit, and watch as they prepared him for death.

Ella sat on the chair in the corner and waited for Sammy's daughter, Mindy, to come into the room. Mindy had left his side when they were moving him from the Intensive Care Unit (ICU) to this room, where they were waiting for him to die.

No one had ever told Ella how long they anticipated he might linger, after the machine was detached that fed his lungs the life-giving oxygen. They told her his brain was no longer functioning so the signals for breathing were hit or miss at this stage of his life, or non-life, depending on how you wanted to look at it.

After about a half hour, Ella walked into the hall and dialed Mindy's cell phone number. No response was forthcoming.

Ella waited a few more minutes, anger building inside of her because she couldn't locate Mindy. She walked around the hospital checking areas where she thought Mindy might be waiting, but to no avail. Ella couldn't find Mindy anywhere.

The RN had instructed Ella to go to the admissions office. She had to complete the necessary paperwork to get her husband's body transported from one state to another, and directed toward the funeral home that would be his last resting place before the final descent into the ground.

By the time Ella completed the paperwork, she was so angry with Mindy's disappearance that she walked out to her car, slumped in the seat, and finally cried. When Ella was alone and responsible for the chores, it was hard to get the crying done. She really needed to cry more than anybody could know.

Ella started the car and took off, away from the place of pain. She needed to go home and mourn for her husband, her love, and her life. The mourning part of this scenario started many months earlier, when Ella accepted the realization that her husband was living on borrowed time due to a severe heart condition, diabetes, and other complications that come with both of those maladies. She thought those problems would be the reason his life would end. As it turned out, a colonoscopy, a simple procedure that neither he nor Ella feared in the least, was what prompted a coma ending in death.

Ella wasn't worried about Mindy and her cousin, Martha, who was her traveling companion. They had made their way to the hospital. She was quite sure they would be able to make their way back home and out of her life forever.

Of course, Ella was wrong. Approximately two hours after she arrived at her lonely house, the two young ladies were standing in her doorway.

Ella welcomed them to enter, cursing under her breath at the same time.

If they wanted an apology from Ella, they weren't going to get one. That wasn't the first time Ella had that very same thought.

Over the twenty-five years Ella was married to Mindy's father, his four children from his first marriage had treated Ella like dirt. You would have thought they would have gotten used to Ella being around, but they didn't. So Ella didn't want to be around them.

She never stopped them from visiting their father, and she provided meals and beds when needed for all who came. Her only request was that they not travel in packs. She accommodated twenty-five visitors one weekend, traveling in five separate cars. She made it perfectly clear to her husband that she would never do that again. She was expecting five people, not five carloads. She spent the entire weekend cooking and washing dishes. By the time they all left, there was no more food in the freezer and no money to restock.

Another time when they visited, every time Ella would walk into a room to join in the conversation, they would rise en masse and exit to the outside, or into the next room. She finally chose to go to her bedroom when the dinner dishes were finished, so she wouldn't be smacked in the face with the obvious exit. That was when her husband discovered the problem.

"I am going to tell them to stop being so ugly with you," Sammy said one evening, after actually seeing them walk out of the room, leaving her sitting alone.

"No, don't bother," Ella told him. "They've been doing this for over twenty years now. They don't see any reason to change and I agree with them."

About a month before Sammy's unexpected death, she suggested he find out when his family was planning another gathering, so that she might drive him to share the fun. Ella needed to be given advance notice, because it was her wish to stay in a motel while he was visiting. She also worked full-time, so scheduling a vacation with her superiors was important.

Like she said, Ella didn't want to see them any more than she had to.

Sometimes it was hard to be nice.

"Mindy, you and Martha can have the back bedroom. You don't mind sharing a bed, do you?" Ella said as nicely as she could muster.

"That's fine, Ella. Is there anything you need me to do?" Mindy asked sweetly.

"No, there are cold cuts and drinks in the fridge. The chips are on top, and the bread is on the counter. If you see anything you want, just help yourself. I've got to make a few phone calls, so I'm going to my bedroom."

Later on that evening they were all making nice in the living room as they gathered around the television.

The next day, Ella's sixtieth birthday, she had to go to the funeral home to make the arrangements, followed by a trip to the cemetery, twenty miles away, to pay for the opening and closing of the grave.

Ella asked both young ladies to go with her. They needed to supply the family information to the funeral director for preparation of the obituary. Ella didn't know how his family tree was branched, and it was way too late for her to even care.

"I don't think I'll have Sandy's name listed," said Mindy.

"Why not?" Ella asked.

"She's not his real daughter. I'm his only real daughter. She was adopted," said Mindy.

"List her name as his daughter, not adopted daughter," Ella told the funeral director.

The coffin was chosen with a military theme, and Ella asked for a military funeral. She knew that would be what he would want.

The viewing was to be the next evening at the funeral home, followed by the funeral the next day.

Ella was so numb during this time. She showed no emotion other than having a blank look on her face, but she was totally aware of what was happening around her.

She was aware that the young ladies had no clothes to wear to the funeral. So before the viewing was to take place, Ella wanted them both to go get something other than blue jeans to wear, as they represented their father's other family.

Ella gave them two hundred dollars in cash, and asked them to give her back whatever they didn't use. She guessed they spent all of it. She never got back a penny. She had used her hospital stash, the money she had hidden away for trips to Roanoke, where he was usually transferred to when his heart acted up. Ella needed it for gas and food. She was never sure when the trips would happen, so she always had to be prepared. She cut down on the expenses by sleeping in her car, many nights.

She was the only family member present to accept condolences in the room with her husband. Ella's sons, Sammy's stepsons, couldn't be with her. One brother had to drive over hundred miles to the airport to pick up the other brother, who was flying in from a Midwestern state with his long-time girlfriend of twenty years. Her sons loved their stepdad very much, and they were both going to share the loss with Ella.

Mindy chose to stay out of the room and speak with no one. Martha stayed with Mindy.

When it came time to leave so the funeral home people could lock up for the night, Mindy decided to visit her father.

"Martha, go get her out of there. These people want to go home. She had all evening to do this," Ella said angrily.

Martha left Ella for a few moments and returned. "She won't leave."

"Come with me," Ella said to Martha.

Ella grabbed Mindy by one arm and motioned for Martha to get her other arm.

"Let's go, Mindy. These people want to go home," Ella said angrily.

Mindy decided life would be unbearable without the father she rarely saw. She sobbed as she started to crumple to the floor and

Ella held her up, dragging her to the door, pushing her through it. She did fall to the ground when she hit the cool air of the night.

"I hate you," she shouted at Ella. "You moved him to Virginia, away from his family and those who loved him. You had him for twenty-five years, and I didn't."

"Stop it, Mindy. You could have visited him more often in those twenty-five years. Where were you? If he had stayed with you and yours, he would have been dead ten years ago. I know that, and you know that. So shut up and get in the car," Ella said, shaking Mindy with all of her might.

When they arrived at the house Mindy went directly to the back bedroom. Ella didn't see her until the next morning, when she rushed past Ella with her suitcase in hand and out the door.

Ella was left alone, and uncertain about anything and everything.

Her friends and coworkers had supplied enough food to feed his enormous family, so Ella was expecting her tiny house to be flooded with people.

A few relatives stopped by before the funeral, but left immediately when they found out that Mindy was not there.

Ella was so alone. The day of the funeral and no family members were with her. No friends called to offer a shoulder, and she was hit smack in the face with reality. She was on her own.

Both of her sons and their girlfriends arrived about an hour before they had to leave to get all of the pomp and circumstance over with at the funeral home and cemetery, so they could go on with the need to grieve.

Ella wore a blank expression during all of it. She was too numb to think about crying. His death had been such a shock, she had to yet to accept it. Ella was going through the motions for some other Sammy. It certainly couldn't have been her Sammy, not her Sammy.

The service was to be held in the chapel at the funeral home. The music was supplied by Randy, who owned the local music store. He played the piano with grace and affection for Sammy, Ella, and all of those in attendance.

The preacher, who lived two houses down from Ella, spoke all the right words.

Both of her sons wanted to be pallbearers, and she mentioned that fact to the funeral director.

"We don't need them. We already have enough," he replied, in an irritated tone.

Ella didn't want to cause a disturbance, so she let sleeping dogs lie. Later, she was so sorry she did that.

While they were waiting for the ceremony to begin, there was a stir of voices. No one could find Mindy.

"Sir, what is the hold-up?" Ella asked. She was growing more and more anxious.

"His daughter isn't here."

"Go on without her," Ella instructed. "She knew when to be here."

No, that was not going to happen. The funeral director took it upon himself to delay the start until Mindy decided to make an appearance.

Ella and her sons were the only representatives of her side of the family. Half of the chapel was filled with many of Sammy's family members, and most of the offspring of his first marriage (minus Mindy).

Ella thanked God and the Stillwell County Schools Central Office, for filling in and representing her and her sons. They were there to support Ella, and they did it well.

She expected trouble to arise at the cemetery from Sammy's three sons and one daughter, because they wanted everything he owned. They were there to drag it off to God knows where. They forgot that everything he owned, Ella owned. Ella had made it perfectly clear that if she didn't want them to have something, they weren't going to get it. She had heard rumblings about how they were going to take what they wanted. That wasn't going to happen. Everything that Sammy and Ella possessed was acquired during their marriage. Nothing was carried over from his previous life.

Trouble was averted when Sammy's family saw the number of people representing her and her sons. If her honorary family members had not joined the caravan to the cemetery, and then remained at the cemetery until her sons and Ella were gone, she was sure trouble would have happened in the form of loud, ugly words and possibly fists flying.

Mindy had expressed the desire to keep the American flag that was removed from atop Sammy's casket.

Ella acquiesced and explained it like this, "Mindy, you were part of his life when he was a soldier. I was not. I didn't meet him and love him until many years later. I think you should have the flag. Speak to me after the service and I will give it to you."

Mindy did not speak to Ella after the service or, for that matter, ever again. She did send one of her sons over to Ella, to get the flag for her. Ella wouldn't let him have it. She needed Mindy to come to speak to her. Mindy didn't come near her.

Ella kept the flag.

As soon as the ceremony ended, Ella told her sons to go to her house and eat with her. She still had hopes that some of his family would stop in for a visit.

Her sons, their girlfriends, and Ella enjoyed each other's company. No one else had enough respect to wish their father's, uncle's, or cousin's widow any condolences.

Ella thought it was over with his family, but she was so wrong.

Her oldest son's girlfriend worked as a cleaning lady, at the motel about fifteen miles from Stillwell.

It seemed that most of the pallbearers had stayed the night and had a drinking party, with pizza being delivered a couple of times during the night.

They trashed the place before returning to Ohio.

Ella knew that her sons and she were Sammy's second family, but they were his second family for twenty-five years.

Wasn't that long enough to accept them?

All she knew for sure, at that point, was that when she buried her husband, she buried his family with him.

Ella didn't want to do that. She didn't want to sever those ties completely.

She loved her husband very much. Ella accepted him, thus she accepted his family. It was a shame they didn't accept her and her sons.

Then, Ella was alone.

Ella's youngest son and his girlfriend returned to their home, many miles away, and made it a point to call her once a week. Occasionally he forgot, but that was okay. She knew that if she needed him in an emergency, he would be there.

Her eldest son tried to stop in to see her on his day off from work. He was a coal miner, and was scheduled to work in the evening when Ella was home from work. His girlfriend popped in once in a while, and that was something Ella truly appreciated.

Most of Ella's life was solitary. Because of her need to care for her ailing husband every non-working hour of every day, she had no friends with whom she could go to the movies, go shopping, or just kill time. There just wasn't any time for anyone else, she was sorry to say.

She had no church family to rely on for support. Sammy wasn't able to sit through a sermon, and Ella wouldn't go to church without him. Maybe she should have, but Sammy was her priority. Ella knew that God understood.

Her advice to anyone who has had to devote his or her life to caring for a family member was to remember that you need a life after that loved one has passed on.

The despair of loneliness could be overwhelming.

Almost a year had passed. The flag Ella held on to at the funeral service was in a box, along with the flag from Sammy's father's funeral service. She would mail them to Mindy with the family photographs that had been sent to him over the years.

Even though she had not heard a word from her, Ella still believed Mindy should have the flag because she was a part of her father's life when he was a soldier.

Ella later changed her mind and she did not mail the flag and photos.

CHAPTER 23
A SHAM

"My life is a sham," Ella said softly. She tried to hold back the wave of tears that were building up behind her eyes. The sudden urge to cry was never going to go away, but she didn't think she wanted it to completely disappear. That pain kept her feet firmly planted on the ground. It made her realize how vulnerable human beings were, and that it could all end just as quickly as it began.

"Don't say that, Ella. Don't give up," Dreama, her best friend, told her in one of their daily telephone conversations.

"The smile that I have to plaster on my face everyday is a lie, a complete phony. I'm not happy, and I doubt that I ever will be again," the sobs were starting and she was angry with herself.

"It will get better, Ella. Just give it some time," said Dreama.

"How much time? It's been almost a year. How much more time has to pass before it stops hurting so much?" Ella snapped back, knowing that it wasn't Dreama's fault. Ella was not able to control the harshness of her voice. "I've got to go, Dreama. I hear people in the hallway," she lied.

Ella heard no one making noise in the hallway, but she knew she couldn't talk anymore because of the gut-wrenching sobs that were trying to explode from her inner being, her very soul.

None of her coworkers or friends had lost a spouse. They had never been subjected to the overwhelming loneliness that consumed the heart. She replayed the last day of spending time with Sammy over and over again in her mind.

***

"Ella, my colon test is scheduled for day after tomorrow. I have to start watching what I eat and following the food schedule today," said Sammy.

"Yes, I know. I've put the canned soups out on the counter that you can eat. The Jell-O is in the fridge. While I'm at work, stick to the diet, okay?" urged Ella.

"Okay. I'm sure going to get hungry for chewing real food," said Sammy.

"I know, Honey, but you have to do it," said Ella.

When they arrived at the Veterans Administration Hospital two days later, the medical people were upset with him because he had not stopped taking his blood thinner early enough, and his blood was still too thin.

Rather than send him back and reschedule the procedure at a later date, they kept him in a holding room overnight so they could perform the colonoscopy the next morning. They gave him six bags of plasma to eliminate the thin blood problem, and said he should be ready for the procedure the next day.

Sammy wasn't so sure.

"Ella, maybe we should just forget about this thing," said a disappointed Sammy as he contemplated going to the beckoning comfort of their Habitat-built home in Stillwell County.

"It's up to you, Babe, but you would have to go through not eating real food all over again, not to mention all the laxative potions you have to endure," said Ella.

Ella wished she had told him to get out of that bed and get into the car—but she hadn't.

Now she was trying to get over the guilt of not encouraging him to go home. Ella was trying to survive the horrendous pain of losing her reason for living.

He had become the center of her life. She worked every day at her full-time job, but every hour that she wasn't working was filled with caring for or sharing her life with her husband, her companion, her friend.

The sham was the phony smile and the "I'm just fine" statement she said to anyone who asked. They really didn't want to know the truth. "How are you?" was a substitute for "hello."

Ella's way of dealing with Sammy's death had been to remove all reminders of him from her sight. She kept herself away from the loneliness of her empty house as much as possible, by scheduling as many book events as possible.

On one of her uglier days last week when she had gone home after work, she decided if she had to die by her own hand, she wanted to slip off into oblivion during her sleep.

That's how Sammy died. They anesthetized him, and he slipped into a coma. He felt no pain.

Ella didn't plan to do that yet, but if she felt the need, that's how she would do it.

That decision was made and her smile returned, for at least a little while.

Chapter 24
WORDS THAT CUT TO THE BONE

In one quick motion, with one click of the mouse, Ella removed from her computer the ugly, derogatory words written about her across the screen.

> Ella,
> Who are you trying to fool? I know you didn't love him that much. Quit trying to convince everyone that you lost your one and only true love.
> Signed,
> One Who Knows the Truth

Why would anyone be so cruel? What did I do to deserve those mean-spirited words? thought Ella angrily.

Even though she had clicked the mouse and removed the words from her computer screen, she knew they were still shining brightly for all with access to the blog to see.

Why would "Truth" let words like that see the light of day? Even if it were true, why say it? That's the type of statement and thought that should be kept private and unspoken, thought Ella.

Sammy had been sick for a very long time, but they were getting by. He knew Ella loved him, or she would have sent him back to his blood-sucking family years earlier.

She was not very demonstrative when it came to public displays of affection. She was not the happy-go-lucky, friendly sort that he was. Ella was one to sit back and watch what was going on around her, which was the complete opposite of Sammy. He would jump into the interaction with both feet.

Ella could control her pain and grief most of the time. Outward signs of her anguish burst forth only during private times. Occasionally she would slip, and those around her could see the tears that she tried so hard to hold back. Ella didn't like herself when that happened. It made her feel vulnerable.

That was not the first time that words cut her to the bone.

"Penny, Sammy almost didn't make it. They had to fly him in a helicopter from Stillwell County Hospital to Roanoke. He's still in intensive care."

"Ella, let's be honest, wouldn't you be better off if he didn't make it?" asked Penny.

Ella blinked back the tears and said nothing.

How could she answer Penny? Ella thought.

Had Ella thought those same thoughts? Sure she had, but as long as she didn't give those thoughts the sounds of life, no one would ever know they had entered her mind.

Now it was coming up on a year since his departure from Ella's life. She was still grieving, maybe not so hard and not so strong, but the pain was still there.

Why would Truth say Ella didn't love Sammy that much?

Who was Truth?

Ella powered her computer down. She wanted to forget about those ugly words.

She went to work and searched the faces of her coworkers, looking for a tell-tale sign of betrayal.

"Maggie, you know I loved Sammy, don't you?" asked Ella.

"Of course I do, Ella. That's a stupid question to ask me," said Maggie.

"Have you logged on to the Stillwell gossip blog today?" asked Ella.

"No. I haven't had the time. I don't check it daily. It usually has something on there that makes me really mad," answered Maggie.

"Make sure you look at it today. I want you to tell me who would write those mean words about me and Sammy," urged Ella.

Fortunately, none of her coworkers flinched under her questioning glance. She was so glad they weren't the source of those hurtful words.

Ella's mind went back to the funeral.

The only person who showed herself was Mindy, Sammy's daughter from his first marriage.

Mindy and her cousin Martha stayed in Ella's home until the morning of the funeral service. The night before the service, at the wake, she screamed at Ella and made a scene that Ella would never, ever forget.

"You took him away from us. You moved him three hundred miles away so we couldn't see him, and he couldn't be my dad anymore. I hate you, Ella. You didn't deserve him. He should have stayed with us," Mindy bellowed, as she sat down on the pavement outside the front door of the funeral home.

Ella grabbed Mindy's arms and pulled.

"Martha, you get behind her and push so we can get her to the car," Ella instructed.

They got her to a standing position and pointed her toward the car.

When the boohooing stopped, Ella answered her venomous words.

"The door was always open for any of you to visit your father. Your three brothers were welcome along with you, anytime. All I asked was that you not travel here in herds. I can't handle five carloads of people, all at the same time, for the entire weekend, like you expected me to do when we first moved to Stillwell. There was a total of twenty-five of you to feed and look after. All I did was cook and wash dishes. It was too hard on your father. Too many people were jockeying for his attention. It took him a while to get over that visit."

"You took him away from us," Mindy mumbled.

"If he had stayed with you and your folks in Ohio, he would have been dead ten years ago. Now straighten up and get over it, Mindy. After all, we were married for twenty-five years. You should have gotten used to my being around," Ella said harshly, as she bit back the bitter sob of anger.

It had been almost a year since that bitter scene. Ella had not heard one word from any of Sammy's family. When his body was buried, Ella's life as his wife was also buried, in the eyes of his first family.

Truthfully, Ella was glad she no longer had to deal with people who didn't like her. On the other hand, after twenty-five years, why couldn't they care just a little bit?

Her phone rang and startled her out of her funeral memories.

"This is Ella. May I help you?" said Ella.

"Who would do that, Ella?" Maggie asked.

"I don't know, Maggie. I just don't know," said Ella.

Ella managed to get through the day without accusing anyone she worked with of being cruel to her.

At home, she approached her computer with trepidation. She didn't want to give Truth the satisfaction of a response, but she needed to do it just the same.

The blog appeared on the computer screen and those words screamed at her.

Truth,
You and I need to correspond one on one. My words are
not for the world to see. Email me at eholcombe.com as
soon as possible.
Signed,
Ella

Ella didn't really expect any further blogging from Truth. The
damage was done. Her only hope was that Truth would reveal his
or her identity if they began an actual email correspondence.

A couple of weeks passed with no more blogging from Truth,
nor was there an email. It appeared her challenge was going to
pass unanswered.

Ella,
What did you do with all of that insurance money?
Can you lend me a little of it?
Signed,
One Who Knows the Truth

Ella's reply:

To: One Who Knows NOTHING,
I used it to bury my husband and pay some bills. There
is nothing left, Mindy.
Signed,
Ella

She heard no more about her unbelievable love for Sammy, on
the blog or through her email address.

"Maggie, it was Mindy, Sammy's daughter. She is still trying
to punish me for taking Sammy away from her. She just couldn't
believe I loved him that much. Maybe she thinks that because she
feels guilty for not loving him enough. But now it's over, she will

probably plan an attack this time next year on the second anniversary of his death."

"Let's hope not, Ella," said a sad Maggie, as she shook her head from side to side.

"We'll see," Ella said softly.

CHAPTER 25
ACCEPTANCE

After the passing of her husband, Ella tried to force herself to cut a path into the world that would allow her to thrive without the love and protection of her Sammy.

It was so hard.

Ella was so alone.

Day to day life without Sammy was almost unbearable, at times. Those times led to many gut-wrenching sobs and pleading questions about why God allowed this to happen.

Ella would never understand why Sammy died when he did. She guessed she should be grateful that he slid into a coma and on into death without ever knowing what happened.

She had fought too many battles with doctors who were willing to let him die each time he had a horrific heart event. She knew in her heart she would have accepted his death much more readily, if it was related directly to a problem with his heart.

Still, to this day, she couldn't understand why Sammy had to die upon the completion of a colonoscopy.

God knew she missed Sammy.

God knew she wondered, *why then?*

But life went on, and Ella had to move on.

The winter was long, in her mind. She couldn't get out and join the world. Even though more times than not, she was alone in a crowd.

People seemed to avoid her. They didn't know what to say about the loss she had suffered, or if the tears would start flowing, gushing forth, at the mention of his name.

Yes, there were moments when that could have happened, but there were also moments when Ella needed a friend to talk to about how much her life had changed, like it or not.

CHAPTER 26
THE MOVIE TICKETS

Ella remembered the auction and the loving purchases she made.

***

About a million times over the last few years, Ella knew she had heard the auctioneer chant the same words many times, as she worked away at her clerking duties for an employer and friend. Strangely enough, she was always on the business side of the auction; therefore, she wasn't able to join in on the bidding process. She couldn't be the recipient of a purchase that might or might not be a fantastic deal.

This time it was different. This time, Ella got to play.

"The bid is ten-ten-ten; will anyone bid twelve-fifty? Twelve-fifty? Twelve-fifty?" said the auctioneer as he looked around the room.

Ella raised her paddle to bid twelve-fifty.

"Twelve-fifty, twelve-fifty, anybody want to make it fifteen? Fifteen? Bid fifteen?" he said as he tried to urge those people standing in front of him to meet his price.

"Sold, for twelve-fifty," he said. The young lady helping him handed Ella an envelope containing two movie tickets that included the popcorn and drinks, worth twenty dollars, for the movie house just down the street from where she lived.

Ella was so proud of her purchase. She knew Sammy would like to go to the movies. It had been a long time since they had enjoyed a movie together.

Then, a set of two tickets for a theater about fifteen miles from them went up for bid. Ella got both tickets for seven-fifty. That's the price of one ticket alone.

Now they could go to the movies twice.

Ella could hardly wait to tell him. After all, the only reason she was actually bidding on things she didn't need was because Tammy asked her to help with the auction fundraiser for the Parent Teacher Association, at the school where Tammy was the secretary and the mother of two young children who attended the school.

Ella really didn't have the money to waste, but she did it anyway. She wanted the two of them to go out into the outside world, to enjoy the waning years of their lives together.

Most people Ella spoke with didn't consider early sixties as waning years, but with Sammy and his bad heart, tomorrow could be his last day—or perhaps even today.

Ella tucked the tickets away into her handbag to wait for a movie to start that they really wanted to see. She was really planning to use the tickets during the coming holiday season. Driving to a movie theater would give them a chance to go out and see all the lights that would be shining from many of the homes in their small town.

She made the purchase on a Saturday, in late October. Sammy went to the hospital on Tuesday, for a colonoscopy that was performed on Wednesday. That very same Wednesday, Sammy went into a coma following that simple procedure. He never woke up.

Now she guessed she would give those tickets to Eddy, her son, and his girlfriend.

Hopefully they would enjoy going to the movies over the holidays.

Ella didn't think she could do it, now. Not all alone.

CHAPTER 27
IF I'D KNOWN

"I never would have purchased this house if I'd known it was filled with trials and tribulations that no human should have to bear," Ella told God in a whisper.

The day she found out that the house was theirs, she believed she was the happiest person alive. Her husband, Sammy, came in a close second on happiness.

"God, thank you, thank you," Ella prayed.

It was a Habitat-built home, so the monthly payment was affordable. Of course, the structure was volunteer-built, so it contained small signs of imperfections in every room, such as a light switch that tilted at a slight angle. Ella loved the imperfections because they were placed in her home by imperfect people, just like her and Sammy,

The reason they qualified for the opportunity to get this house was because of Sammy's total and complete disability, due to a bad heart, a bad back, and diabetes.

It sure was strange that as soon as they moved into the new house, Sammy's heart started acting up big time.

His sickness, with the required out-of-town hospital trips, doctor visits, and many, many medical prescriptions, soon ran them out of savings and they were living paycheck to paycheck on the income from her job and his meager Social Security Disability dole.

"God, don't take Sammy away from me," Ella prayed as she sat in the intensive care waiting room. She needed the doctors to tell her they had gained control over his congestive heart failure, which caused fluid to pour from his nose and mouth, making it almost impossible for Sammy to breathe because of fluid-filled lungs.

Sammy fought that battle and won, but his luck was truly beginning to fade.

"God, what am I going to do about these bills?" Ella pleaded on one of her desperate evenings when she was trying to make her money stretch as far as she possibly could. It was becoming more and more obvious that bills and money were never going to balance. Being sick had cost a lot of money. Trying to help a loved one stay alive was devastating.

"God, I don't want to file bankruptcy, but the lawyer tells me that is about the only choice I have," Ella sobbed, thinking about how quickly her happy days had ended and were followed by despair.

Sammy and Ella filed bankruptcy, and once again, they were starting over with a clean slate.

It seemed that Sammy's health was improving a bit. Enough that he was told he needed to have a colonoscopy test performed, to find out if he was having any problems in his colon that might be causing a bleeding problem. He seemed to mysteriously require blood transfusions, for an unknown reason.

Of course they knew all medical procedures carried a risk, but they didn't really think of a colonoscopy as a life-threatening medical test.

"Dear God, why did you take my Sammy?" Ella sobbed as she tried to come to terms with the fact that a medical test ended his life, and a good portion of her life as well.

Maybe it's unreasonable for Ella to blame the house for all of her misfortune. Yes, it probably was, but she would rather blame the house than put the blame on God.

"God, I know you probably don't want me to say or even think it, but I hope I get an opportunity to put an end to the bad influence this house has on people, and me in particular. That's why tomorrow I'm setting it on fire. Amen."

Ella awoke with a start.

Why would she dream about burning down her house?

Ella didn't burn down her house; now it was hers, lock, stock, and barrel.

It was finally paid for, and unencumbered with a mortgage.

God knew Ella didn't mean it.

CHAPTER 28
SAMMY'S LAST ROLE

Ella watched him breathe. That was probably a description a new mother would give as she watched her newborn take in and exhale each soft breath. Ella did that when her boys were babies, so she knew how it felt.

This was different.

Ella was watching her husband, the man with whom she had shared twenty-five years, breathe in and out with the help of a machine that was keeping him alive.

Hospital sitting had become her second job, the first being a purchase order clerk for Stillwell County Public Schools.

Sammy's many illnesses had kept her visiting hospitals in Stillwell and Roanoke, in Virginia, along with a hospital and the Veterans Administration Hospital in the neighboring state.

If Ella wasn't working or trying to work every week day, life on the road to doctors and hospitals would have been much easier to handle. Unfortunately, that wasn't the case. If she couldn't get to work to fulfill her responsibilities during regular working hours, she would go in on evenings or weekends, whenever she arrived home from the hospital, in order to keep the flow of work traveling through the system.

Ella cared about her job, and she cared about whether or not she did it well. She also cared about the hospitalization she needed to help keep her Sammy alive.

Worry was constantly with Ella, and it was wearing away at her resolve. She needed to do something to keep her mind and fingers busy. Added to her problems was the fact that she had stopped smoking when Sammy had his first heart attack. In order to make sure he didn't return to smoking, Ella had to make sure that she was no longer smoking, as an added incentive for him to stay on the wagon. Ella could truthfully say there were days when she wanted to beg for a cigarette from a complete stranger. She was that stressed.

Crocheting kept her aging fingers and the joints in her hands and arms agile, so Ella carried a tote bag filled with yarn, a pattern, a pencil, scissors, and a crochet hook.

When the crocheting was not in the picture, she also carried with her a pad or two of paper, pens, and writing prompts so she could steer her mind away from the lingering possibility that Sammy might die.

Ella had faced the possibility of his death many times. The most memorable trip to the hospital occurred when he had a flash attack of congestive heart failure.

She watched in horror as fluid drained from Sammy's nose and mouth. He struggled to breathe from lungs that were full to the point of running over with liquid.

Even though she lived very close to the hospital, about a mile away, she was afraid she wouldn't be able to get him there alive without help.

The paramedics loaded him up immediately and red-lighted him to the emergency room.

After a short time, the medical personnel told her to call in his family and asked her if he had a living will.

"No," Ella responded angrily. "You will do everything possible to save him, please, and then transfer him to Roanoke where his heart doctor can take care of him. He is way too young for you to let him die without a fight. Fifty-nine is not old enough to die."

Roanoke Memorial Hospital kept him alive, and she was able to take him home a week later.

Ella would have accepted his loss that time as inevitable.

His breathing was even and smooth, machine-made, not the breaths of her Sammy, who snored and suffered from sleep apnea. There would be a sudden intake of air, then a holding period where he would not intake or exhale, until finally there was a loud exhale. That was the signal that she, too, could breathe again. Her breath was usually a sigh of relief, because she knew there would be another intake, followed by an exhale, in Sammy-like fashion.

Smooth, even breathing patterns, as the machine forced intakes and exhales, were the sounds coming from Sammy then.

Ella picked up her crocheting, but her fingers weren't busy enough to keep her thoughts off of the machine that was breathing for Sammy.

She laid the yarn aside, and picked up a pen and spiral-bound notepad to move her mind away from the rhythmic sound.

She thought about her writings, mystery novels and several books of nonfiction, about her life and the lives of others who asked her to tell their stories.

Ella wrote many short stories, with the thought of incorporating them into the guts of a novel or nonfiction book at a later date. In the meantime, she would use those short writings as entries into short story contests, to see how she measured up against other writers.

The mysteries she had been writing each time she sat at the hospital had been stories of Ella (disguised as Mary Ella), and included Sammy in each one, in one form or another, along the way. He may have had a different name, but he was a vital part of each story.

Ella took a break from her racing thoughts to stare at her Sammy. She was looking for some kind of life other than the machine that was gently pushing his chest up and down with each intake and exhale of air.

She was working on a novel, the fourth one of the Mary Ella series. She would use it to write Sammy out of her life. Like it or not, that was going to happen.

Ella had tried to keep her novels up to that point in time upbeat and real, meaning that even though they were tales envisioned in her imagination, they could have happened. In many cases, some of the occurrences spun as yarns of fiction were based on reality, with only the names changed to protect Ella from lawsuits.

When she started novel number four of the Mary Ella series, she knew in her heart it would be the last one in which Sammy would play a large role. She started the book before he was admitted to the Veterans Administration Hospital for a colonoscopy, and she knew that his life was coming to an end. She just didn't know how it would happen, or if maybe she would be joining him, taking her last breath possibly due to a devastating car accident.

They had fought the fight for over twenty of their twenty-five years together, trying to keep him upright, on his feet, and alive.

This was the final battle.

Ella watched him and the machine.

She cursed herself for not making him go home with her when she had the chance.

"They said my blood is too thin because of the blood thinners I have to take for my heart. I did stop taking them three days ago, like I was told, but it's still too thin," said her exasperated husband.

"Are we going to have to go back home, put you through the regimen of cleaning out your system again, and come back in here at a later date?" Ella asked with that very same feeling of exasperation.

"No, they told me I could stay here overnight and they would transfuse me with plasma to thicken my blood. They'll do the colonoscopy the first thing tomorrow morning. What do you think I should do?" Sammy asked her.

Ella didn't give him and answer. She let him make the decision.

She wanted him to stay in the hospital and get the procedure over and done with, so they could go on with their lives. She knew the doctors were looking for the reason he needed blood transfusions so often. They had an idea that he was bleeding somewhere in his body, but the location of blood loss had not been determined. Maybe the colonoscopy would find it.

He chose the Veterans Administration Hospital to perform the test, because it would be easier on her pocketbook. In addition, he was a veteran and he felt more comfortable among veterans.

The doctors packed him up, blood-wise, with plasma. Of course, that thickened his blood.

They performed the test and moved him to recovery, where he had his heart attack. This time his death was not inevitable, and she did not willingly accept it.

No one could ever get her to believe that those doctors weren't the reason he was in this condition. He was on blood thinners for a reason. When they thickened his blood they crossed over the line, and it turned his blood to the sludge that couldn't travel through his corroded veins and arteries.

Ella was not at the hospital when he was taken away for the procedure. She was on the telephone with him at that time, waiting for the furnace man to finish checking their furnace at home, which was about a hundred miles away, give or take, from the hospital.

She jumped into the car as soon as the furnace man completed his inspection and drove to the hospital with the feeling, again, that she'd made a mistake. She should have been there. Deep in her heart, she knew she should have been there with Sammy.

When Ella arrived at the hospital, she walked to the room where Sammy had stayed overnight. She knew he probably wouldn't return to the same room, because he would be released after he had spent time in recovery.

Of course he wasn't in that room, so Ella went searching. The information desk was the only place for her to go, hoping to get an actual answer as to where he was.

"Could you tell me where Sammy Holcombe is?" Ella asked the busy information clerk.

"Spell the last name, please," commanded the not-so-kind sounding man behind the desk.

"H-O-L-C-O-M-B-E, Sammy," Ella said calmly, hoping he would follow her lead.

"ICU, Room 6," he blurted out as he tried to dismiss her.

"Where is ICU?" Ella asked. She didn't have enough sense about her to question that he was in ICU. He had spent many times in that specific department in different hospitals, in the past.

She'd followed the clerk's verbal instructions that led her to this room where she was sitting, watching her Sammy breathe with the help of a machine.

The shock of seeing Sammy in a coma threw her for a loop, but she was alone, as was usual, and she had to find out what happened.

A doctor entered the room, along with some medical students. The doctor danced around her questions, not wanting to give her any answers he did not have.

The fact that Sammy had a heart attack in recovery was explained to Ella. There wasn't much hope for survival. He went too long without oxygen to the brain, as well as his heart. The defibrillator inside his chest went off six times and didn't revive him, so they got him onto the machine that was doing his breathing.

The next morning, Ella drove back to the hospital in the neighboring state from her home in Stillwell, Virginia, her heart filled with dread. She had been told to go home the previous evening, and they said they would call her if need be during the night. They didn't call, so he was still holding his own, or so Ella thought.

When she arrived at his cubicle in ICU, she discovered how wrong she was.

Sammy was no longer lying on that bed, quietly breathing through the machine.

Now his arms were rising up on each side to a ninety-degree angle, his eyes were springing open, his arms would smash back down against his bed, and his eyes would close. This movement was repeated over and over again. It didn't stop until he was given medication that shoved him deeper into the coma.

That sudden arm movement and eyes flying open made Ella think he was improving, but dear God, he had to stop that eventually, didn't he?

Stopping would not happen until he was given the medication to stop the warped impulses from his brain.

After some words of explanation from the doctor, she was made aware of the fact that his brain was no longer functioning normally.

The arm and eye movements were signs of impending doom.

In other words, Ella was watching her Sammy die.

A few days later, she was forced to make the decision.

Ella did it when she had to. It was the third time she had to watch someone die, and the second time she had to tell them to pull the plug.

She had endured a near miss when her fifteen-year-old son was hit by a car. At that time, Ella didn't know whether she should pray for him to live or die.

He would not have wanted to survive as a vegetable, without a working brain, legs, or arms. At that time in her life, the question of living or dying was totally in God's hands. There was no way Ella could make that decision.

The doctors weren't sure of what his outcome would be, and nothing could be determined until he climbed out of his coma.

He survived, and as a family, they survived his traumatic brain injury.

No decision was made by Ella, except that she prayed for the best for her son. What else could she do? Ella was his mom.

Her push to write had basically taken hold when she was with Sammy during all of his hospital stays. Ella would sit at his bedside or in a waiting room, and busy her brain with another totally different life. In other words, her people in her novels were doing other things, not sitting in hospitals like Ella.

Several times in the past, she had seen him wake up and lie there quietly, so as not to disrupt her train of thought.

Ella's writing turned from happy, uplifting stories to death and dying revelations. There was nothing she could do about it. That need to relive the death and dying was there in her heart and soul, and it had to run its course.

She was finally able to finish the fourth novel of the Mary Ella series, and she wrote Sammy out of her writing life—a little.

This writing has told you that he continued to jump into Ella's writing. She saw his smiling face, with his bright, blue eyes surrounded with crinkles of joy, every day, if only in her mind.

He always encouraged Ella to write and supported her by traveling with her to events that didn't consume all of his strength. Ella would say no to events that would take her too far away from home or had extended, tiresome hours, because he wanted to travel with her. If she had signed up for one of the time-intensive events, he would have gone with her, or she would have had to fight to make him stay home.

Ella missed his physical company, but she knew he would always be looking over her shoulder, pushing her to achieve her writing goals.

His illness forced Ella to do what she had always dreamed of doing, and that was to write.

Ella guessed he knew she would need something to cling to, when he was no longer of this world.

This ability to forecast her future needs pushed him up into the sky, to rank on par with her father, whom she'd always considered the smartest man she ever knew.

Ella's dad had more common sense and real life knowledge than anyone she had ever known.

Ella missed his ability to make bad things go away with a word or two.

He was stern and hard sometimes, but his decisions were made to protect her. It just took her a while to realize that.

As an adult, Ella could look back at those points in time when he really made her angry and could finally smile.

He was so right.

To this day, she longed to hug her dad's neck and thank him for making her the strong person that she was, and for being in her life.

The ability to use her imagination to create alternate worlds to explore changed her life forever, and was always encouraged by her Sammy, even after death.

CHAPTER 29
PICK IT UP, PLEASE!

Ella volunteered for various nonprofits as she looked for her niche. Her main objective was to find friends, not a replacement for Sammy, but she found it hard to convince others.

***

Ella started collecting secrets when she was just six years old. Perhaps she could find another this day, as she helped the Ladies' Auxiliary at the hospital in her small town of Stillwell.

"Ella, you can work on that stack of junk over there in the corner," Mary said as she pointed to an unsightly pile of personal belongings from someone's life.

"Sure, okay," Ella said, as she grimaced at the stack to be sorted and distributed to the correct areas of the garage, where everything was being stored until the day of the yard sale.

I shouldn't grumble, Ella thought, *I volunteered to help in any way I could.*

Clothes, shoes, curtains, dishes, pots, and pans were haphazardly piled into the boxes and then unceremoniously dropped into the corner furthest away from the shelves and bins.

Maybe they are trying to tell me something by making me walk so much, Ella thought as she glanced down at her oversized, round body.

"Just shut up, Ella, and get it finished now," she told herself gruffly.

Ella spoke the words out loud, and managed to get a lot of quizzical glances from others walking near her.

She talked to herself a lot since her husband died. It was mainly because she was almost always alone.

Retirement didn't help her with combating all of the alone time, but she definitely didn't miss the daily grind of trying to make the boss happy.

Oh well, Ella thought, *I'm not the first person to ever talk to herself, and I'm sure I won't be the last.*

She picked up a pair of jeans and searched the pockets for items that shouldn't be in there.

She felt something; a piece of paper, folded up and shoved to the very tip of the front pocket.

Ella pulled at the small, folded paper and began the process of straightening it so she could read it. She wanted to find a secret; not that she wanted one to tell anyone else, but it would be interesting to know a hidden fact about one of her neighbors. That way she could smile a knowing smile when she bumped into them, and move on letting them wonder. She might even put the event in her next novel.

Her jaw dropped when she started reading the handwritten words, letters written in bold, black, permanent ink.

To the Person Who Finds Me:
I'm so tired of being lonely, with nothing or nobody to live for each day. I don't want to go on any more.
Please forgive me,
Larry Questor

Ella knew a Larry Questor, but she hadn't seen him for a while. She hoped that he hadn't ended his life, especially from loneliness. She had thought about doing the same thing, once or twice. She wasn't desperate enough or brave enough to carry out the act.

She kept the note, and vowed that she would look up Larry Questor. She really wanted to talk with him, if he was still among the living. She wanted him to know that loneliness was not a good enough reason to end it all.

Ella worked about another hour, finally reaching the bottom of the stack.

She drove home with her mind completely focused on trying to locate Larry Questor.

She greeted her three cats at the front door, and performed her kitty obligations of feeding her feline children.

Then it was on to her next routine step, turning on her computer. While it did its thing of booting up, Ella located her telephone book.

Ella looked up Questor, Larry, in the white pages. No listing—that meant he probably had an unlisted number.

She decided to search through the small pieces of paper in her handbag. She thought he'd given her his card, when she saw him last. She was a little old-fashioned, and did not call him at that time. She felt that if he wanted to talk with her, he could call her at the numbers she had handed him, imprinted on her business card.

"There it is!" Ella shouted, as she grabbed the piece of paper on which his phone number was printed.

Ella dialed the number and held her breath.

"Come on, Larry, pick it up, please," Ella mumbled as she heard the phone ring and ring.

After the tenth ring without an answer, she headed to her computer.

She was going to enter his name into the search engine, to see if she could find anything important listed about him that was out there for the world to see.

The world of the Internet seemed to be filled with Larry Questors. She was surprised to see so many men with the same name.

The next step was Larry Questor, followed by Virginia. Another batch of items popped up, but not as many as for Larry Questor alone.

Ella couldn't find any references that led her to believe any of the Larry Questors she was seeing was the one for which she was searching.

Then it occurred to her that he could be from West Virginia. Her little town was located less than twenty miles from the state line. Maybe she was looking in the wrong state.

Larry Questor and West Virginia took her to a reference to a school teacher.

"That's him!" Ella shouted, which made her cats look at her to see what was going to happen to them. Usually when Ella raised her voice, it was because she was after them for one reason or another, but mostly for scratching and sharpening their claws on her furniture.

Ella continued to scan through the references and saw nothing that indicated he was dead.

Her husband's obituary could be found referenced to his name. She knew if Larry Questor had died, an obituary would have been published, and it would be referenced somewhere in the Internet world.

She breathed a sigh of relief when she did not find a listing for his next of kin.

At least he's still alive, Ella thought. She returned to the easy chair next to her phone, so she could try his phone number again— if she had the right number. Hopefully he hadn't changed his number, or cancelled his service as many people were doing nowadays, giving up a land line for only the cellular phone connection.

She punched in the numbers and waited.

"Hello," said Larry, as he struggled to gain control of his breathing.

"Larry Questor, is that you" Ella asked.

"Yeah, this is Larry. Who am I talking to?" he asked. He continued to try to control his breathing.

"It doesn't sound like you, Larry," Ella said.

"Been running to get to the phone. Who is this?" he demanded.

"Ella Holcombe. You met me at the Arts Center," Ella explained.

"Oh yeah, right. How are you, Ella?" he asked, a little more courtesy flavoring his tone of voice.

"I'm fine, but I wanted to know, how you are doing?" Ella asked softly.

"What do you mean?" he asked.

"Well, I heard you endured an ugly divorce, and then you were forced into retirement. I know you didn't want to retire. You weren't ready yet. So, how are you doing?" Ella said again.

There was a long pause filled with silence, so much silence that Ella thought he had disconnected the line.

"I'm okay, Ella. I don't like being retired and alone all the time, so I went back to teaching, as a substitute. I get called out a couple of times a week to fill in for absent teachers. Things are a lot better now. Thank you for asking," he said.

"I'm so glad you're okay. I don't want anything else from you. I just want to know you're okay," Ella said.

"Why?" he asked.

Ella didn't want to tell him she had found his note. She didn't want him to know that she had discovered that deep, dark secret from his past. She didn't want to tell him that she, too, had had those same thoughts, but not because of the death of a marriage.

Ella had lost her partner, her husband, her lover of twenty-five years, when his heart failed to work.

She knew when she first met Larry, he thought she was husband hunting. Her husband had passed on about two months earlier, but finding a replacement for Sammy was the furthest thing from Ella's mind.

It had been over a year since he died, and Ella was still not looking for a replacement; a little companionship and/or conversation, but nothing permanent.

Just like Larry, she was afraid of the word permanent, but not because it might be a relationship that would end in divorce or death. On the contrary, Ella did not want to watch another man die.

"Larry, I'll see you when you stop in the Arts Center the next time, for one of the receptions. It's time for me to go. Bye," Ella said, in a rush of words.

Ella hung up the telephone and smiled. It felt good to know that Larry Questor was still alive.

Hopefully, Ella would see him again at the Arts Center. If not, she hoped life treated him well.

CHAPTER 30
I'M NOT READY

"You need to go out, Ella. You deserve a little company. You know Sammy would want you to find someone else," said the voice of a dear friend.

"Yes, I know, but I'm not ready," Ella said firmly, in response.

"When will you be ready? It's been over a year," Patty probed.

"I don't know, Patty," Ella said.

"This guy I want you to meet is really nice. His wife died a while back. He's like you because he's alone," urged Patty.

"Let me think about it," Ella said, as she tried to hide her irritation.

Ella hung up the receiver and fought the urge to cry.

She was not looking for a replacement for Sammy. Yes, she was living a lonely existence, and there were times when she really, really would have liked to share her time and space with someone. But, and this was a big but, Ella was not ready to change her life again.

When Sammy's heart stopped struggling with trying to keep the precious blood flowing through his veins, Ella's life changed abruptly.

She no longer had to schedule every waking hour based on how her beloved Sammy was feeling that day. Many times she awoke early in the morning, her thoughts clouded with the feeling that there was something wrong. Ella knew she wasn't going to get through the day without one of the many, many trips to the emergency room and yet she had to work. Ella had tasks that had to be done, regardless of Sammy's ill health.

Ella was always on an adrenaline high that kept her on her feet and going.

After the funeral, the adrenaline was completely drained and Ella was alone.

As a writer, Ella needed time alone to get her thoughts together so she could put them into the computer, and eventually on the printed page.

Now Ella had all the time in the world to do just that, but she didn't want to do it. Her mind was addicted to the adrenaline and the push, push, push to snatch moments here and there to write.

Ella needed more clutter, more appointments, more reasons to get out of bed every morning, but that didn't mean she had to have a new man in her life.

Work, the daily grind, was good and wonderful during the week. Ella knew she had a reason to wake up, for five days each week. That wasn't saying she didn't miss Sammy during those five days, because she did. When her workday was done, she would go home to endure each evening, filled with her salty tears of despair and loneliness.

The need to take care of Fred, Sammy's dog, and her three cats allowed her some companionship. Ella found herself talking to the animals a lot.

Depression set in big time each Saturday and Sunday. She thought she would go crazy during the winter months.

Spring showed up, finally, and Ella started going places, setting up her book displays to sell her books.

Ella scheduled library appearances, craft shows, fairs, festivals, and book signing events to fill up the lonely hours of each weekend.

She had developed a new love in her life, and that was the need to sell her books and become recognized for the writer that she was, and the better one that she would be in the future.

Ella was not ready to change her life again. She liked what she was doing now—most of the time.

"Ella, did you think about going out?" asked Patty.

"Yes. I thought about it, over and over again," said Ella.

"Well, what's your answer?" pushed Patty.

"My answer is no, not just yet," said Ella.

"You're making a mistake. Sammy would want you to go on living your life," urged Patty.

"Yes, he would, but that's not the reason, not completely," said Ella.

"What is the reason? I told you the man is a gentleman, a really nice and wonderful person," said Patty.

"I know. Everyone I've talked to who knows him says the same thing. It has nothing to do with him. He's ready to find a wife replacement, but I'm not ready to be that replacement." Ella said.

"It's just a date, Ella."

"No, Patty, it's an audition that I'm not ready for. My life changed drastically, several months ago. I've accepted the change. I actually learned to like the change and maybe even love it, most of it anyway. There are still times when I cry—a lot."

"Okay, Ella, maybe later."

"Maybe not at all, but that might change, too. Who knows what's lying in wait for me?" Ella said, with an apologetic smile.

CHAPTER 31
THE BLIND DATE

Ella was daydreaming at her desk. She was thinking about happier times, which almost always included Sammy, when the phone rang.

"I've talked to Greg, and he would still like to meet you. I told you before that he's really a nice man," said Patty, without even a hello.

"I know, I know, but I still don't think I'm ready," Ella said.

"I'm going to give your number to Greg so he can call you," said an exasperated Patty.

"All right, I'll talk to him if it will make you happy," Ella said.

"He'll call you later today," said Patty.

"You sure are in a rush," Ella added.

"Aren't you tired of being alone all the time?" Patty continued.

"Well, yes," Ella answered honestly.

"Then it's settled. Greg will call you. See you soon," she said cheerfully.

Ella continued to work and was interrupted by a ringing phone.

"Hello?" Ella said politely.

"Hello, is this Ella Holcombe?" said an almost shy voice.

"Yes, it is."

"I am Greg Barnett. Patty's friend," he added.

"Oh yes, she said you would be calling," Ella said. She tried to sound interested.

"Patty has told me so much about you. Would you like to go to dinner this Saturday night?" he said in a flurry of words.

"No, not Saturday. My son is coming for dinner. Perhaps on Friday?" Ella asked hoping in her heart that he was going to be busy.

"Not good for me. I'll be at my son's house that day. Would Saturday the next weekend be okay? Are you free that night?" he probed.

Ella paused as she thought it over. She had promised Patty.

"Yes, that's fine. What time?" Ella asked.

"I'll pick you up at four o'clock. I like to eat early," he said, almost sternly.

"I do, too," Ella said, not sure that what she was doing was a good thing.

"I'll call later in the week and get directions to your home," he said, then disconnected the line.

Ella hung up the phone, shaking her head.

She didn't hear from Greg for a few days, so she figured the date was off and she no longer had to worry about it. Ella was at work when an unwanted call disturbed her.

***

"Hello?" Ella said, glancing at the caller ID.

"Ella, this is Greg. I need the directions to your house," he said in a business-like tone.

"Sure, do you know how to get to Grant's on Riverside?" Ella asked.

"Yes, of course," he replied.

"I live on the next street over, in front of Grants. I can see their sign from my living room. My house number is 305," Ella answered in the same professional tone.

"No problem. I'll pick you up Saturday at four," he continued.

"Sure," Ella said

The line was dead, so she hung up the phone and stared at it.

Patty called Ella's office, in her normally cheerful mood.

"Greg is direct, isn't he?" Ella asked.

"Yes, but I thought you would like that about him," she answered.

"Well, yes, I like direct people. I'm a direct person, as you well know, but there is no foreplay involved in his conversations with me," Ella said skeptically.

"What are you talking about, Ella?" Patty asked.

"He makes me think that talking to me is a business function that needs to be completed in a rush. There have been no words of introduction, other than being a friend of yours. He makes me think talking to me is a gigantic chore for him," Ella explained.

"That's just the way he is. You'll like him when you get to know him," she coaxed.

"Maybe so, but I still think this is a mistake," Ella mumbled.

Ella was pacing and mumbling. She had the horrible feeling that she was making a horrendous mistake. She hoped this wasn't a waste of time.

***

A knock at the door stirred her from her doubtful thoughts. Ella opened the door slowly.

"Hello, Ella, are you ready?"

"Don't you want to come in?" Ella asked.

"No thanks. Let's get going. I'm driving to Princeton to Ryan's. Do you like Ryan's?" he asked.

"Yes. You know, there's a Ryan's in Bluefield. That's a lot closer," Ella urged.

"I like the one in Princeton better," he said.

"Okay, whatever you want," she said agreeably.

They didn't talk much as they sat next to each other in the car. He didn't seem to mind the silence and, truthfully, neither did Ella. When they were seated at the table inside Ryan's, Ella finally started to talk. The silence was getting to her.

"You've known Patty for a while," Ella stated, trying to break the ice.

"Yes, I did a lot of the inside work on her new house that she and Randy had built," he answered. His face was covered with a prideful smile.

"Oh, that's good. I have been inside her home and it is beautiful," Ella said, praising his work.

"How long have you known Patty and Randy?" Greg asked.

"A number of years. I did some work for Patty as a side job, but now we are just close friends," Ella said.

"Yes, she told me that. Have you been to this Ryan's before?" he asked, as he abruptly changed the subject.

"No, my husband and I always went to the Bluefield location. I haven't been there since he died. I just don't like to go to that kind of restaurant alone, if you know what I mean," Ella answered solemnly.

"How long ago did your husband pass on?" Greg asked.

"About a year."

"My wife died about three years ago. You do know I'm eighty years old," he said sternly.

"Yes, sir, and I'm sixty-two. Is that a problem?" Ella asked.

"Not for me. My wife was a good woman. She died of cancer. She always liked this restaurant. That's why I like to come here. She was my third wife. All of my previous wives passed on while I was married to them," he explained in a rapid burst of words.

"You miss her don't you? Your third wife, I mean," Ella said.

"Do you miss your husband?" he snapped back at her.

"Yes, I do," Ella answered without a second thought.

Only small talk came from either of them on the drive back home. When they arrived at Ella's house, she did not ask him to come in, nor did he show any indication that he wanted to enter her world.

Ella crawled into bed with a smile on her face.

***

"How did the date go?" Patty asked not even trying to hide her excitement over the telephone the next evening.

"It was probably my first and last one, with him," Ella answered. She tried to hide her smile.

"Why?" asked Patty.

"I'm not ready to replace his wife, and I'm sure he knows it. This was more like an audition than a date. He kept dwelling on his dead wives, all three of them," Ella explained.

"If he calls you again, will you go out with him?" Patty asked.

"No, I don't think so. He's still too attached to his last dead wife's memory. She was his third wife, and he has outlived them all. I'm too attached to Sammy's memory, and I made sure he knew that. It didn't seem like a good omen when he told me all of his previous wives had died," Ella explained with a shudder.

"Greg's wife died. Sammy died. So what? You have to go on living," Patty said.

"Yes, Sammy died, but my two previous husbands were alive and kicking the last time I saw them. Makes me think Greg is the reason all of his wives are dead. Kind of spooky to think about, isn't it?"

"That's not fair, Ella," stammered Patty.

"Maybe not, but I'm not ready to watch another husband die before my eyes and I definitely don't want to be the fourth wife that Greg outlives," Ella said as she shuddered again.

"You really weren't impressed with him, were you?" asked Patty.

"No. I wasn't impressed, but don't blame him. All I could do was find fault. That doesn't make him a bad guy. I told you I wasn't ready. I guess that was true. I'll get there eventually, but not yet. I'm not ready yet."

Chapter 32
UNKNOWN

Unknown was all Ella ever saw on her caller ID at two o'clock in the morning.

Why was Unknown calling her, and hanging up without leaving a message to explain her abrupt awakening?

Ella had questioned everyone she knew about an unexplained need to reach her at two in the morning. Of course, they all denied such a stupid stunt. Many of them acted as if she were accusing them. No amount of explaining would clear the air. So Ella had to let the inquisitions die without finding an answer

She really wanted to get the phone company to trace the call so she could put a stop to the nightly interruptions, but she was afraid it might cause more trouble than it was worth.

What if it were a friend of hers, playing a prank? Would she want to get him or her arrested? Well, maybe, depending on who it was and why.

Ella tried the *69 trick, but that didn't get her anywhere. The line was blocked, so she could not call the number back, leaving her at a dead end.

"Hello," Ella whispered sleepily, knowing that this annoyance was going to end up as a dial tone, like it always did.

"Ella?" said a distorted voice.

"Yes? Who is this?" she demanded, wide awake with the mention of her name.

There was static crackling on the line and nothing else.

Suddenly the dial tone roared in her ear. The conversation was over. Ella was to hear no more utterances, no words of explanation, no apology.

The sound of the phone ringing in the middle of the night was shock enough to her nervous system, without getting into the fact that she was wide awake when she replaced the receiver on its cradle. She knew it would take her an hour or more to settle down and fall into a restless slumber.

The lack of restful sleep was wearing on Ella.

She was a new widow, in that her husband had been dead for a little over a year. Ella was trying very hard to learn to live alone. She remembered times in her not-too-distant past when she prayed for a few hours alone. Now, Ella prayed for someone to ring her doorbell or call her on the phone; the same phone that she cursed at two o'clock every night. Ella had discovered that living alone, traveling alone, and always being just one wasn't what it was cracked up to be.

She had never been one to worry and wonder about what bad thing might be lying in wait for her.

Now, with the sudden nightly calls, she had become afraid of always being alone. What if someone were meaning to do her harm? Was that what was happening?

No, she didn't think so. Her gut told her that wasn't what was happening. Her gut failed to tell her the reason for the phone calls, however.

Ella longed for a peaceful, uninterrupted night of blissful sleep, but her mind told her that was not going to happen.

The tell-tale signs of restless sleep were showing up on her face, in the form of dark circles that continued to deepen with each passing night.

"Ella, are you sick?" asked a concerned coworker.

"No, not really. I just haven't been sleeping well, that's all," Ella answered lazily as she fought the urge to drop off in mid-conversation.

"What's keeping you awake?" asked the coworker.

"A phone call. Always at the same time. Always after I drop off into a sound sleep," answered Ella tiredly.

"Who is calling you?" asked the coworker.

"I don't know. They usually don't say anything, except for this last time, last night," said Ella.

"What was said last night?" the coworker asked.

"He called me by my name. He called me Ella."

"What else?" probed her coworker.

"Nothing else. Then the line went dead, followed by the blaring dial tone. I wish I knew who was doing this to me. It's beginning to scare me a bit," said Ella.

"It should scare you. It's got to be someone you know, or he wouldn't have called you by name. It is a he, isn't it?" asked the coworker.

"I think so. There's so much static on the line that it's really hard to tell," said Ella.

"Does the voice sound familiar?" the coworker asked.

Ella paused before answering. She wanted to think about what she was going to say. Back in the deep, dark recesses of her mind, she knew she had heard that voice before, many, many times before; but how was she going to tell her coworker the true identity without appearing to be a crazy person?

"No, I mean yes. Oh, well, what I meant to say is that I haven't been able to tell much from only one word, and that being my name," Ella lied.

"Yes, I guess that would be a problem. How long has this been going on?" continued her coworker.

"It started about a month ago," replied Ella.

"This has been going on for a month?" asked the astonished coworker.

"Yes, it has," said Ella.

"No wonder you're tired. Have you called the phone company to get a trace started?"

"No, I didn't want to get anybody into trouble. It could be a friend playing trick on me," said Ella.

"Ella, whoever is doing this is not a friend. You should get them into trouble. No friend of mine had better do anything this stupid to me. I mean it."

"You're right. I guess I should have the call traced," said Ella.

Her workday finally ended and she drove home to wait for the inevitable phone call. Ella made herself stay awake, even though all she wanted to do was to stretch out on the sofa as soon as she walked through her front door.

Ella was one of those people who couldn't take naps. It interfered with her ability to sleep later that night. She needed no more interference—only sleep.

Of course, it wasn't only the two o'clock phone calls that were keeping Ella awake. She finally had to face facts about her inability to get past her husband's sudden departure from her life, and move on with living.

God help her, but Ella thought she was looking forward to the two o'clock wake-up calls so she would know that someone wanted or needed her, even if it was the middle of the night.

That's crazy talk and Ella knew it, but she thought the despair of loneliness could do that to anybody, especially her. Her family, at one time, consisted of six individuals living in a three-bedroom mobile home, in a trailer park. Now, she was all that was left. Her mother died. Her husband died. Eddy, her eldest son, moved into his own home, which he was sharing with his girlfriend. Aaron, her youngest, and his Becky moved to a Midwestern state.

She had tried to give herself a good talking to, on a couple of occasions.

"Ella, Sammy is dead and gone," she would tell herself. "It's time you moved on. He wouldn't want you to give up on living. So get out, meet people, do things, and keep on living."

That talk worked for a day or two, and then Ella would remember why she was so alone. The private crying would begin again.

Those around her commented on her strength.

She wanted to shout back, "I'm not strong. Help me get over this!"

Ella didn't. She swallowed her words, held back her tears, and forced a weak smile onto her weary face.

The people she worked with avoided any and all conversations that even hinted at the loss of her husband. They couldn't or wouldn't understand that Ella needed to talk. She needed to let it all out. Ella needed to tell the whole world how much she loved her husband.

There it is.

The r-r-r-ing.

Will he talk to me?

Will he tell me why he's calling me?

Will he tell me who he is?

Ella grabbed the telephone. She wasn't sleeping. She was waiting for the call.

"Hello," she whispered.

Static.

"Hello? Please talk to me," Ella pleaded.

Static.

"I know who you are. Talk to me, now!" Ella demanded.

"Ella?"

"Yes, yes, it's me. I'm Ella."

"Forget about..."

"What? Forget about what?"

"Go on with your life..."

"I can't," Ella cried.

"You have to..."

"No!" Ella screamed through the sobs. "Who are you?"

"Unknown," was the reply.

Ella hung up the telephone and fell into a deep, dreamless sleep.

The alarm sounded at five o'clock, but she didn't hear it. Ella never opened her eyes until ten o'clock. By then, she was already two and a half hours late for work. She blinked her eyes, not believing the time that was in bold, red numbers, right in front of her.

"Jen, I'll be there in about an hour," Ella explained to the young lady who answered the telephone. "I just woke up," she sputtered. "I've never overslept before. I'll be there as soon as I can."

"Take your time, Ella. Is everything okay?"

"Yes. I think it is," she answered.

"You sound different. What happened?" asked Jen.

"I slept," Ella replied.

She showered, dressed, and went to work with a legitimate smile on her face. It wasn't one of those smiles you forced to your lips and kept there, even though it hurt.

When Ella walked into her little office on the second floor, she whispered a little prayer, "Thanks, Unknown, for letting me move on."

CHAPTER 33
CONTENTMENT

The coffee was gone, but the warm feeling of contentment was still with her. It wasn't going to last long, that feeling of contentment.

Her world was changing rapidly without any input of her own, which might have redirected the course.

Ella was a widow, and that was a sudden change. A few months ago, she was a married woman with a mountain of medical bills and a wonderful husband who had accumulated those medical bills.

Now, Ella was sitting in a cafeteria in a mall, watching all the people around her as they talked to each other and lived lives that didn't involve her.

The coffee made her feel content, but the fact that she was always eating alone shattered that contentment on occasion. If she didn't ponder the aloneness, if she just did what she liked to do, the very same thing she had liked to do most of her life, and that was people watch, she was OK. Ella didn't have to interact with them. She sort of eavesdropped on snippets of conversation, and watched the facial expressions of those sitting one table away from her, or completely across the room.

People-watching used to be a pleasurable pastime that Ella would choose to do. Now, it was a permanent solitary task. She had no one sitting across the table from her, with whom she could share her commentaries or criticisms.

Two tables away and to the right, Ella saw an older lady sitting ramrod straight, picking up her fork and pushing the food it held up and over to her mouth at a ninety-degree angle. That was the way she had seen the young cadets eating in a military school, in a movie many years earlier.

The woman did not smile, but instead concentrated entirely on feeding herself in such an unorthodox manner.

Across from her was a blonde-haired woman, who appeared to be permanently attached to the cellphone she was holding in one hand while she used the other to rapidly load her mouth with small bites of food. She continued to chew and talk on the cellphone until she completely cleared her plate. Then she was up and gone, with her food eaten and her cellphone closed.

And of course, there was Ella. She was sitting at a table that would accommodate a party of four. Ella was trying not to be conspicuous. She was trying not to be so miserably alone. She was trying so hard to convince passersby that she was alone at her choosing.

Ella couldn't abide the pity, the same pity she foisted upon the lady eating at ninety-degree angles. The cellphone user didn't deserve her pity. The party on the other end of the conversation probably needed the pity, for having to listen to all the chewing, slurping, and smacking of lips.

"Would you like a refill, ma'am?" asked the sweet young thing serving the tables.

"Yes, please," Ella answered. The server poured the hot coffee into her cup.

Ella surrounded the cup with her fingers. She hoisted the cream-colored utensil containing the reason for her momentary contentment to her lips. She could feel the smile forming inside. She wasn't quite sure if the smile came through to the outside world.

CHAPTER 34
PEOPLE WATCHING

Ella was doing it again. She was people-watching in a popular cafeteria, where there seemed to be a constant flow of bodies in and out as they hurried on to meet the demands of their busy lives.

An elderly couple, with the gentleman riding in a wheelchair, seemed to be the happiest of those sitting at tables within her line of sight.

The gentleman, Ella called him John, was wearing an oxygen hose on his face to enhance his ability to breathe the good, warm air. It was filled with food smells, caused by the cooking of the fine cuisine for which the restaurant was famous.

The little gray-haired lady, Ella called her Mary, made sure everything that John wanted to eat was within his reach. She did not baby John at all, but she made life a little easier for the disabled man.

Mary kept a good stream of conversation going, using a pleasant, calm voice at all times.

When she finished her meal, she sat at the table and patiently waited for her companion, John, to place his utensils on the plate and reach for his cup of decaf coffee.

She talked to him, and he answered with short sentences or one word. She looked at him with old eyes, displaying a love of many years.

Mary, a petite lady of about five feet or less, gathered up everything and started pushing John's wheelchair to the exit.

Ella jumped up to open the door, allowing them to leave without the struggle that would have occurred without her assistance. It made Ella's heart feel good to help.

This cafeteria seemed to be the place for families and friends. They outnumbered the solitary diners, much to her chagrin, because on many occasions since the passing of her husband, Ella was not a solitary diner by choice.

She also saw the servers who had not been called upon to take care of people at the tables rushing to decorate the interior of the restaurant with Santas, snowmen, and poinsettias to highlight the coming holiday season. In no time at all, they had created a Christmas atmosphere filled with laughter and joy.

Joy was hard for Ella this year. Sammy, her beloved husband, companion, travel mate, and best friend, succumbed to a life-ending colonoscopy three weeks before Thanksgiving a year ago, one day before Ella's sixtieth birthday, less than two months before the Christmas holiday.

She was sitting behind a table filled with the books she was trying to sell, in order to meet the obligations incurred while trying to keep her husband alive.

Ella struggled to force a smile on her face to overcome the black, empty feeling that filled her heart.

She was trying so hard not to think about her reasons for sadness, but Sammy would never, ever leave her thoughts.

Her eyes were tearing up again. She had to force her thoughts away from her Sammy and how much she missed him.

Ella saw a single soul sitting at a table on her left side. Ella called the man Jim. He appeared to be a gruff individual, with a no-nonsense attitude. He wasn't wearing a wedding band. With a man the absence of a band wasn't unusual, even if he still had a wonderful wife sitting at home.

He must have asked to speak to the cafeteria manager. He drummed the fingers of both hands on the table, looking irritated and unhappy.

"He's busy right at this moment, but he will be out to speak with you in a few minutes," explained a noticeably nervous server.

"That's all right," said Jim to the busy waitress. "If he is too busy to talk to me, I understand."

"Sir, if you can wait, he will be out to talk to you."

"I'm busy, too. I'm eating right now, so I'm not going anywhere."

He continued to eat, stopping every so often to drum his fingers and look gruff.

"He's still busy, but he will be here to speak with you soon," whispered the worried waitress.

He could see the worry on her face and he reached out to her, grabbing at her arm. "Don't worry, Honey, it's not about you."

The tension melted from the waitress with those words.

Jim continued to eat and drum his fingers. When he finished his meal, he sat and waited, drumming his fingers.

"Do you know the manager's name?" he asked the same harried waitress.

"Yes, sir, his name is Donald Androsis."

"Can you spell that last name for me?"

"A-N-D-R-O-S-I-S," she said distinctly, so Jim could write it down on the small piece of paper he was holding.

"Where is your main office?"

"Alabama."

"Do you have that address?"

"No, sir, but the lady at the cash register may have it."

He stood up and started to put on his coat. He had to pause to let diners carrying food-filled trays to pass.

He saw Ella watching him.

"Busy corner here," he said in a booming voice.

"Yes, it is. It's kind of dangerous to cross the oncoming traffic," Ella said with a smile.

He crossed the isle and stood in front of her table, still filled with books.

"I'm a local author. I have a book of Christmas stories you need to buy for your wife or girlfriend."

"I wish I had one," Jim said as he shrugged his shoulders and walked away.

He stopped at the cash register near the exit to pay for his meal, and said a little too loudly, "Do you have the address for the main office in Alabama?"

"No, sir, but you can find it on the Internet."

"Thank you, young lady," he said. He finally left, after having stirred up several employees with what everyone believed to be a complaint. He never did get to speak to the manager, who was extremely busy with all the extra holiday traffic being served in his cafeteria.

Ella was sure the home office would get the complaint, whatever it was. Jim appeared to be a man who, like a dog with a bone, would chew away at something until he felt relieved or too tired to continue chewing.

It was mid-afternoon and the traffic pattern was beginning to slow. It wouldn't last long because the evening meal rush would rev up traffic momentarily.

Ella hadn't had much success at selling her books. Only two had been purchased so far, but she considered it a winning experience if she sold just one. Two books sold made it a double win.

The pause gave her time to reflect upon the nice young men she'd encountered when she made her trips to her parked car to retrieve her selling materials.

The first young man, of what appeared to be Asian descent, stood with the door handle in his hand, waiting for Ella to get closer before he yanked the heavy glass and metal door. The show of respect floored her, especially coming from a young man she did not know.

As she exited the mall to get her second load of books, another young college-age man held the door for her. Ella smiled at him warmly, and nodded to acknowledge his kindness.

It didn't take a lot to impress Ella. Both of those young men were appreciated by this little old lady.

While she was contemplating the unexpected signs of respect, her small book selling table was surrounded by people, looking at the pictures in the collage she'd prepared to spark interest in her mystery novel.

Ella guessed it was a good idea. She had one of those every once in a while.

Two more books were purchased, bringing her to a total of four out the door, so far.

The cafeteria was full of people who needed to complete their chores, not waste time with an old lady trying to foist her novels onto unsuspecting victims.

Ella was beginning to feel better about being there, until she was told that it was snowing outside and the roads were getting hard to manage.

She waited and worried about what the roads would be like when she left after four more hours.

Another lull in cafeteria traffic happened, but not before two more precious volumes of her words were sold.

It was usually a terrific book signing if she could sell ten books. Ella was well on her way to terrific.

The booths and tables were filling up again. The all-day shoppers were tired and hungry. The new arrivals were anxious to get eating out of the way, so they could go explore the Christmas wonders for sale throughout the mall.

Ella was tired of sitting behind the table. She got up and stretched her legs. A trip to the ladies' room was the only exercise she would be getting until she hit the magic hour of eight o'clock, when she could pack up and drive for an hour and a half to her home in Stillwell. Hopefully it would only take her that long, ninety minutes, but the falling snow might prolong the long, lonely drive.

Another book was purchased, this time by a man. He actually bought one of the anthologies she was prone to giving away when someone bought two of her novels. It served as an added incentive, a simple come-on that worked once in a while.

Another book gone; this time, it was her first novel. The total was now at eight. Ella was keeping her fingers crossed. She had about two more hours to reach the magic number of ten.

The looky-loos had appeared at the table several times today. Most told her "I don't have time to read," which in a few cases might have been true. Most of the time it was just a dishonest way of telling her they were not interested, or they didn't have the money. She would have rather heard the truth.

Ella looked at the live poinsettias on the half-wall partition that separated this large room into two sections. Those deep red leaves reminded her of her mother, and her mother's love for the Christmas plant.

Her mom didn't inspire too many good memories, because of the way she acted a few years prior to her death. Old age made her mean and ugly when dealing with Ella. That attitude was the opposite of the mom who raised her.

It was nice to have a good memory about her mother's love for poinsettias.

A lady sitting at the table directly in front of Ella was chatting with a woman who looked to be her mother. There was a strong facial resemblance.

The younger woman, Ella called her Jill, was blessed with a beautiful face. She had a quiet, subtle beauty that radiated from her.

"I hope you weren't embarrassed by my stares," Ella said, as Jill began to walk toward the exit. "I think you are so very pretty," Ella added in explanation.

"Thank you," was her humble reply.

She looked at Ella's books, questioning her about each volume. Jill chose two and Ella gave her the third, an anthology that contained her prize-winning short story.

Ella's total was ten sold and one given free at that point. She had a terrific book signing, with the possibility of selling even more.

"Do you like to read?"

"No, I wish I did," mumbled a lady as she passed Ella's table.

Again Ella asked, "Do you like to read?" A different lady stopped to look, and decided to buy the small volume of Christmas stories.

One more hour needed to pass, so Ella could go out and brave the winter storm during her long drive home.

A nice lady also named Ella quizzed her about her writings. She purchased a book and went on her merry way.

That purchase had exceeded all of her expectations, and made the long drive ahead of her a little more bearable.

Now the area in front of her was thinning out, and Ella saw that two older males sitting in different booths were eating their suppers alone. Both had hair that was mostly white and thinning in spots. Both were nicely attired in clean, casual clothes. Neither of them had on a wedding band, and the lack of a smile on either face told her they spent most of their days and nights alone.

Ella was sure Christmas held the same appeal for them as it did for her. Being alone did not allow for the feeling of great joy.

All the late diners were arriving to eat before they headed for home and hearth.

Suddenly the two diners were lonely no more, and every booth and the tables seemed to be filling up rapidly. The older of the lonely men departed, wearing a scowl across his handsome face.

"Have a good evening," Ella whispered as he passed her table.

"You, too, lady," he told her as he continued to walk to the counter to pay for his food.

You could tell who the frequent visitors to this eating establishment were. After the meal had been consumed, they stacked the individual serving dishes in the same manner the servers did when they bussed the tables.

The second lonely man did just that. He stacked all of his serving dishes before he departed the table without leaving a tip. Ella was sure the stacking was helpful to the servers, but leaving no tip was not kind.

Ella had arrived there at eleven o'clock in the morning, and it was now almost eight o'clock at night. It had been a long but terrific day.

Ella was missing Sammy.

Chapter 35
WAITING FOR CHANGE

Waiting for change always seemed to take a lot longer than Ella expected.

She knew that for a fact. When she married Edward, she waited for him to change.

Well, he did change—but not for the better. He became a full-fledged drunk, so Ella decided she needed to be the one to change.

Ella moved on after five years.

Her life was without a husband for the next eight years. Ella didn't like the utter loneliness. Her sons were her reasons for living, but they couldn't fill the void in her heart that her divorce from Edward had left.

Ella eventually did meet a man, with whom she fell madly in love. He could have been the one. He could have filled that void forever and always. Jack stirred up feelings that she had never felt before he entered into her life.

When Ella met Jack, he and his wife were separated. When Ella decided to change her life, once again because of a man, it was after another five years of frustration and despair had left its mark on her heart.

Ella waited for him to change, but she ended up doing all of the hard work.

During their five years together, Jack was separated from his wife maybe half of the time. They stayed married until years after Ella was no longer part of that triangle.

Ella changed from being the other woman to being a lonely, single mom again.

She left the city where all of the heartache seemed to consume her.

Ella moved on to a small town and met Mike.

Mike swept her off her feet, with his attention to her every wish and the weekly delivery of flowers to the office where she worked as a legal secretary.

"Will you marry me?" came rushing out from him in an excited whisper.

"Yes, Mike, as long as you think the kids will get along," Ella answered apprehensively.

Ella was changing her life one more time. She was going headlong into a family, with a new husband and his two daughters, who were the same ages as Ella's two sons.

Within six months, the daily battles between both sets of kids taught Ella that life was too short for this problem.

Ella was divorced for the second time, vowing that she would never get married again.

Ella returned to loneliness and despair.

Well, that vow of never marrying flew out the window when she met Sammy, who was the love of her life for twenty-five years.

The end of her marriage was a long time coming. It was a change she did not want. He died less than a month after their twenty-fifth wedding anniversary.

Ella wasn't waiting for that change to happen.

It did happen though, and she missed him.

It had been over a year since his death, and Ella was still waiting for a change. That always seemed to take a lot longer than she expected.

Ella wanted to wake up each morning and not miss him so much that it hurt.

The change would get there eventually. Ella hoped she lived long enough to experience it.

Ella never wanted to forget about Sammy. She only wanted it to hurt a little less.

That wasn't too much to ask, was it?

CHAPTER 36
I NEED TO GET A LIFE

Ella was so afraid that this was what her life would be like. She had seen this tale of woe in her dreams.

***

The alarm clock trilled its six AM wake-up call. Ella turned off the clock, sat up in bed, and clicked the television's power button. The evening news was getting underway.

Ella stared at the television.

"When did Bruce Williams start doing the local morning broadcast?" she muttered. She struggled to crawl from the tangle of covers that were weighing her down.

"Maybe there was some kind of terrible disaster. Maybe I should pay attention to the broadcast to find out what's going on," Ella said to no one, because she lived alone. She often expressed her words out loud so she could hear the sound of a voice, even if it was only her own.

"Talking to myself is not a sign of insanity, is it? Oh well, if it is, at least, I will be able to talk to people in the crazy house. I won't always be alone like I am now."

Ella had been talked into retirement by some of her coworkers at the Stillwell County School Board Office.

"You've got your time in, Ella. You can just sit at home and enjoy life." said Nancy in encouraging tones.

"I don't know, Nancy. Why would I want to sit at home every day?"

"You earned it," shouted Jackie. "Let someone else take on all of the school system purchasing problems."

"Who wants to do that, Jackie? Do you want to be the purchase order clerk?" Ella snapped. She knew what they were doing. They were trying to move her out to pasture so the younger ladies could take over.

The cluster of ladies separated before more unsettling words were uttered.

"I should have stayed at work. Why did I let them chase me away?" Ella cried.

It wasn't the first time she mumbled those bitter words. That statement would cross her lips daily, as a matter of fact.

"Ella, stop being so silly," she scolded herself. "You need to get yourself together, and make your bed."

The television announced the menu for the prime time line-up.

"My God, what happened to my day?" Ella asked. Worry etched some lines onto her aging face. "I remember turning the alarm off at six AM. Did I go right back to sleep? If I did, why in the world did I sleep a full twelve hours? I've never done that. What happened to me, for twelve hours?"

Ella decided she needed to check herself to see if she had a stroke. Maybe that would explain the loss of such an enormous amount of time.

She peered into the old medicine cabinet mirror, looking for signs of drawing muscles and paralysis. She knew what to look for, because she had watched her mother suffer through several mini strokes before she succumbed to the major stroke, four years later.

"Nothing. I didn't have a stroke," Ella mumbled. "It's horrible to always be alone. I need to get a life."

Ella had volunteered on many different occasions to help escort patients at the community hospital, but that got old and was so very tiring. She had to give up the hospital, because all the seriously ill people reminded her of Sammy's passing. She cried too much.

She stood at the front gate of the local county fair every year, collecting the price of admission from those entering the land of fun. That lasted for a week, and then it was over.

This year the fair wasn't as much fun, for two reasons.

The first and foremost reason for disappointment was that her husband was no longer with her. He'd died a couple of months after last year's fair.

The second reason for less fun was that without her working partner, they stationed her at the back gate to collect admissions. Ella didn't get to laugh and joke with the regulars, because very few people entered the fair through the back gate, between the hours of three and five in the afternoon.

This would probably be the last year Ella would work the fair. She needed to be out front to meet and greet the public. It helped chase away the loneliness.

Now she had nothing left, no reason to get out of bed each day.

Several years earlier, her life and small mobile home was filled with six people. Her mother, her husband, her two sons, and one son's girlfriend filled her life with excitement of one kind or another each day.

First her eldest son, Eddy, moved out to be on his own.

Then her youngest son, Aaron, and Becky, his girlfriend, decided they needed their own space.

Next her mother passed away, leaving only her and Sammy to keep each other company.

Sammy died.

Ella was alone.

The volunteerism was discontinued.

Ella no longer had a reason to get out of bed.

The walls of depression were closing in on her, allowing forgetfulness to take over her mind.

"I need to check my medicine. Maybe I took too much. Maybe that's why I lost twelve hours," Ella whispered. She walked back to her bedroom to check her pill box, marked for daily doses.

"Today is Wednesday. Thursday, Friday, and Saturday should still be in the separate compartments."

Ella popped up the plastic cap marked Wednesday. Empty.

"That's good. It should be empty. That means I took my medicine."

Ella hesitated over the Thursday pocket. Did she really want to know if the pills were gone?

Empty, so she must have taken two days worth of drugs.

Ella moved onto Friday.

"Do I really want to do this?" she asked the four walls that surrounded her.

Instead of popping the Friday compartment open, Ella violently shook the little plastic pill box.

No noise, no rattling of pills could be heard.

"Oh my God, I took the pills for four days!"

Had Ella done that purposely? She suddenly understood how depression could kill her.

"I could have died!" Ella cried.

She took the empty pill box into the kitchen, where she would leave it. Ella would refill the separate compartments and place the box on the top shelf of the cabinet over the sink. She would then have to be awake enough to make herself walk into the kitchen to retrieve her medication. Maybe she would live through the next bout with depression, and skip the trip to death that had been waiting on the sidelines.

This time it was close—too close.

"I need to get a life," Ella whispered again as she got ready to return to her bed. "After all, it's nighttime. That's what you are supposed to do at night, isn't it?"

CHAPTER 37
SMILING AGAIN

Ella woke up this morning with a smile on her face. That was not hard to accept in most cases, but the thought of celebrating another Thanksgiving without Sammy was more than she wanted to bear for the past four holiday seasons.

Today, November 3rd, was the fourth anniversary of his death. Ella was not depressed. She was not crying.

She was smiling because she had discovered her reason for giving thanks and telling the world about it. At least her world, as encompassed by the Bluefield Daily Telegraph, in the article she was submitting for publication.

Ella was so very thankful for the twenty-five years that he shared his life with her.

The twinkle in his bright blue eyes and the shock of dark blonde hair that would fall onto his forehead to be flicked out of the way adorned a face filled with a sincere smile and crinkles of laughter.

Ella was thankful for the ability to look upon his memory with a smile.

The tears had finally ceased. She could mention his name without the forlorn sadness that had overtaken her in the past.

Thank you, Sammy, for all of your support, love, and allowing me to remember you without sadness.

Thank you, God, for allowing me the pleasure of twenty-five years with Sammy.

CHAPTER 38
STARTING OVER—AGAIN

Ella was sitting at a table in front of the gift gallery at Heartwood, the artisan showcase for southwest Virginia. She was waiting for what she hoped was a busload of eager, willing shoppers, who would reach into their pockets and find the money to buy her books and/or afghans.

She was happy to be here, and she felt she had earned the right to do what she liked to do, rather than what she was required to do. Heartwood, through 'Round the Mountain, asked that its members chose at least one day each year to demonstrate his or her craft. Ella was lucky enough to be able to demonstrate her abilities with both areas, literary and fiber arts.

Ella volunteered or paid her way into all of fairs and festivals she could schedule within a one-hundred-mile radius of her home. From April through November, she did her best to fill up every weekend with book sales opportunities.

Heartwood gave her a chance to sell during the week.

The lines got a little fuzzy when Ella tried to explain that she had retired, but she was working harder now than she ever had as she tried to coax people into taking a chance on reading the works of a local writer.

"Hi, I'm a writer from Stillwell," Ella said to a couple who were approaching her table for a look-see. "I write mysteries, short stories, and nonfiction. I will be happy to tell you about any of my twelve books that might interest you," Ella said with a kind smile.

The reply Ella usually received was "You wrote all of these?"

"Yes," Ella said with that same smile.

They glanced at her book offerings, but made no effort to pick one up for a closer inspection.

"We just got here," they said in unison. "We want to look around first. We might be back."

They moved on to look at the rest of the offerings of hand-made items throughout the large facility. These people were referred to by those sitting behind the tables or under the tents as "be-backers." The odds were good that they would not be back.

Ella could either crochet or write to keep herself busy during periods of time when she was not trying to talk to a browser. But she had forgotten the tote bag containing her next angel afghan project, so she would be writing today.

Book number thirteen was already with the publisher, Little Creek Books. It was a young adult novel, set in the mountains, telling the story of a teenage amnesia victim. Ella was waiting for the proofs to be read, so there was nothing to do on that book until a later date.

She had two new mysteries in the works. The first mystery was a story about Mary Ella, a sixty-something lady, who managed to find trouble everywhere she went.

The second mystery was about a single mother of two teenage, twin daughters and a ten-year-old son. She worked as a legal secretary, and managed to lead her friends and her children into fun and sometimes peril. This was the second book of the Lindsay Harris murder mystery series, and Lindsay was off to a new adventure.

Ella also had some nonfiction books in the works. The first on the agenda was a book about the building of her house. Ella owned the first Habitat for Humanity built house in Stillwell County, Virginia.

She and her husband, Sammy, qualified for the house almost fifteen years earlier, because of his health problems and her limited income. She would be eternally grateful to the **committee that chose Sammy and** her to acquire the house. She didn't know what would have happened to them, if they hadn't been able to buy their house through Habitat for Humanity.

The preparation for the book about her house required her to interview the volunteers. They told her of their many antics as they worked on the construction of her house and prepared it for occupation by its first owners, who were not Sammy and Ella, in less than seven days.

Sammy and Ella were not fortunate enough to be the first owners, but they still considered themselves very lucky to get it just the same.

The book that was necessary for her to write was a fictionalization; an account of her love for her husband. He had left her life physically, but would always remain in her heart.

Ella's depiction would include the short writings she'd finally talked him into compiling before his death. They were wonderful stories that always made her smile.

A nonfiction book would be the story of a young woman in Kingsport, Tennessee, who had a remarkable paranormal ability that should be shared with those who were interested.

Today Ella was working on a couple of short writings to be entered into writing competitions, to win the honor of seeing her work in print either on the Internet or on paper.

Ella was busier now than she ever dreamed she would be. She did not want to become a retiree who would vegetate and become a permanent couch potato, especially after her Sammy died several years earlier.

Ella had worked all of her life for other people, but now the picture had changed. She got to work for herself, and she loved it.

CHAPTER 39
ON THE ROAD AGAIN

Ella had heard the phrase "on the road again" in reference to truckers. Now, she had to admit she could identify with its meaning.

When she retired a few years ago, Ella was afraid she would vegetate and become a couch potato. Well, maybe that happened for a couple of days. Ella could see a bleak future full of nothing for her. When the third day arrived, she started moving around to force herself into action.

Ella jumped into her writing and crocheting, switching from one to the other when she became bored with whatever she was working on at the time.

She started scheduling whatever she could to get out and about, and away from the draw of the sofa and vegetation.

As a writer, she made phone calls or sent emails to any likely suspect who would allow her to hold a book signing; or if there was a festival, be it craft or anything of that nature, to set up a table to hawk her wares.

Ella was a widow and she lived alone, human being wise. But she shared her house with her late husband's three cats; Jughead, Cloudy, and Wild Child, not to mention the two vagrants,

Shadow and Blackie, that occupied her front porch a couple of times a day. Once in a while an enormous tomcat, almost all black with touches of white on his feet and huge, yellow eyes, dropped in to visit the food dish. She called him Hulk, and he looked that menacing.

He wasn't the only menacing creature to appear on her front porch. Skunkie was a nightly visitor to the cat plates that contained scraps of leftover food, as well. Ella knew she had to do something about his nightly visits, but she didn't have any idea of what to do. To tell you the truth, she liked Skunkie.

Ella would also get visits from Opie, the opossum, and a raccoon that she hadn't yet given a name.

The cats were taking over her life and she knew that couldn't continue. She had to have human contact, not feline.

Then came winter. Ella couldn't get out much or schedule many appearances, for fear of having to cancel due to inclement weather, but she could write.

Write she did.

Ella finished two works in progress, both mysteries, and edited two books for a friend. She was busy and accomplished a lot, even though it was a daily struggle to stay away from the couch and television.

When the weather started to improve and cancellation of programs and appearances didn't loom over her like a black cloud, Ella started filling up her calendar with choices that were best for her and what she did.

Ella volunteered three to four hours one day a week, at the local community hospital. She did that when she was a teenager, working as a candy striper, hauling patients to and from the physical therapy department. She had always planned to end her working life with an effort to again help in some way. She didn't have the money to give, but she could give them her time.

For years and years Ella had volunteered for the county fair. It only happened one week out of each year. She wanted to see it stick around while she was here, and long after she was gone.

Her newest job was working for the Board of Elections on Election Day, be it spring or fall or both.

This volunteering went along with her book events, which were heavily scheduled from early spring until Christmas, leaving little down time.

Her problem then became not that she would become a couch potato or vegetable; Ella instead struggled with trying to slow down so she wouldn't burn herself out. That was the problem she liked.

Due to time constraints, she resigned from three of her volunteer projects.

She smiled each time she remembered the dread she felt about retirement.

Ella thanked God that she had her health, and could truly enjoy this well-earned change in her life.

Retirement was good!

ABOUT THE AUTHOR

Linda Hudson Hoagland of Tazewell, Virginia, a graduate of Southwest Virginia Community College, has won acclaim for her series of novels including *Snooping Can Be Doggone Deadly, Snooping Can be Devious, Snooping Can Be Contagious, Snooping Can Be Dangerous, The Best Darn Secret, An Awfully Lonely Place, The Backwards House, Death by Computer, Checking on the House,* and *Crooked Road Stalker.* She has also written biographies and stage plays and has had her short stories, essays, and poems published in anthologies including *Cup of Comfort* and *Christmas Blooms.* Her other books include *Watch Out for Eddy, Just a Country Boy: Don Dunford Updated 2014, Living Life for Others, Quilted Memories, 90 Years and Still Going Strong,* a selection of short writings entitled *A Collection of Winners,* and a poetry collection *I Am...Linda Ellen.*

Linda Hudson Hoagland is the 2015 President of the Appalachian Authors Guild.

Hoagland is a retired Tazewell County School Board Purchase Order Clerk where she worked for almost 23 years.

She has two sons, Mike and Matt who are married to Sherry and Becky.

For more information, visit www.lindasbooksandangels.com or email lhhoagland@yahoo.com.

AWARDS

1st Place – Pearl S. Buck Award for Writing for Social Change
West Virginia Writers

1st Place – Sherwood Anderson Short Story Contest

1st Place – Summertime Blues Poetry Contest –
The Storyteller Magazine (Arkansas)

2nd Place – On the Same Page Literary Contest (North Carolina)

3rd Place – Alabama Writers Conclave – Creative Nonfiction

3rd Place – Green River Writers Flash-Fiction Contest – Kentucky

4th Place – Alabama Writers Conclave – Short Story

Honorable Mention – Writer's Digest Popular Fiction Awards/Crime
(National)

Honorable Mention – The Writers' Workshop Hard Times Contest
(North Carolina)

Publication – Poetry Society of Tennessee Northeast Chapter's
Anthology – *Fresh Breath*

Honorable Mention – Tennessee Mountain Writers –
Inspirational Writing

Bluestone Review – Published a poem and short story

Kudzu – Published a short story

A House for Christmas
Published in *The Front Porch* 2004

Contentment*
Published in *Lost State Voices, Volume III* 2010

I'm Not Ready*
Published in *A Magazine for the Arts* 2009

On the Road Again
Published in *West Virginia Writers Newsletter* 2013

People Watching
Published at www.whisperingtree.net 2010

Smiling Again
Published in *Bluefield Daily Telegraph* 2012

The Decision*
Published in *Bluestone Review* 2009

Published in Collection of Winners 2012 by Publish America

COMING SOON

Look for *Onward and Upward* also written by Linda Hoagland. In this story she follows Molly Thompson as she walks through her everyday life with the wonderful good luck of meeting really nice people that she considers angels right here on Earth. Those people didn't have to do extraordinary things, only everyday nice things that turn out right. She doesn't consider herself an angel but she might be wrong. What do you think?